RISE OF THE DOG SOLDIERS

By

Jason Bowles and Lawrence Trujillo

Rise of the Dog Soldiers

TodayIsAGoodDay Media

Cuentos Press
ISBN-13:978-0-9975300-4-9

Book cover design by Dale DeForest

The authors would like to thank all those involved in the editing process.

Foreword

This novel is completely fictional in nature.

Any resemblances to events or persons, living or dead are purely coincidental.

Jason: I dedicate this book to my beautiful wife, Nancy, my amazing boys Jake, Dylan and Ryan, and my parents, family and close friends, who made sure I didn't give up when life got hard. Thanks for all of your support; I am forever grateful.

Lawrence: I dedicate this book to my wife, Sofie, my grand-children, and great-grandchildren of the Laguna and Navajo Tribes, and to the spirit of Dog Soldiers, and all Native American's who fight the good fight.

CHAPTER 1

Daniel Thunder Hawk had his Sirius satellite radio tuned to classic rock, shades on, and the sunroof to his 1999 Ford Explorer wide open. The sun shone brightly and the wind felt great on his face. His long dark hair whipped back and forth in the wind. He took a long pull on his Coke.

Once again fortune had smiled on him. He had made it past the border patrol checkpoints and the cops. As soon as he saw the road sign at the Navajo Nation, he breathed a sigh of relief.

Like always, he was tense from the moment he met his contact near the Mexico/New Mexico border at Santa Teresa, to the point where he entered the reservation.

He now drove through the Navajo Nation, which is the largest Indian reservation in the United States.

With sixteen million acres and twenty-five thousand square miles, it is about the size of West Virginia. Volcanic plugs and cinder cones, domes of rock that form mountains, and breathtaking canyons make the high desert plateau inhabited by the Navajo people among the most interesting locations in the United States.

A mechanic in Mexico had built a specialized hidden compartment into the engine block of Thunder Hawk's Explorer. Drug dealers praised his design. The mechanic spent a lot of time figuring out how to engineer the design to disguise the drugs, where detection dogs could not smell them. It had worked like a charm. Now the radiator was loaded to the brim with white gold, cocaine. And

1

who cared if the illegal cargo was harming the White Man? It was making Thunder Hawk money, easy money, at that.

Thunder Hawk didn't always have money. He had a tough upbringing in the Northern Cheyenne tribe, in Lame Deer, Montana. His dad died, drunk, in a car accident when Thunder Hawk was twelve. As a kid, he watched his dad abuse his mom and siblings. So while his dad's death hurt, it wasn't devastating. Thunder Hawk wasn't all that close to him.

He was closer to his mom. She struggled and worked two jobs cleaning houses and a motel chain to raise her four sons. Sadly, one older son embezzled money from a job and ended up in prison. Two other sons were drunks, and they were in and out of jail.

Thunder Hawk was the youngest and had to learn early on to fend for himself. His mom did her best but in the end, Thunder Hawk had taken the only path that he could.

He was a good basketball player, shooting guard, and was offered a scholarship to a junior college. Unfortunately, the drugs won out. Theft and minor crimes escalated to drugs and fights. He lost his scholarship and dropped out. Without an education, he couldn't find a job.

But right now all of the pain and problems were in the past. He was twenty-two, riding high, the world ahead of him, and making more money than he had ever seen and that didn't hurt with the ladies either.

He had first met the man in a bar in Farmington. Jaime was a chill guy in the back of the bar. Daniel, and a few of his friends, had gone fly fishing earlier in the day on the San Juan River, near Farmington, New Mexico.

Fishing had been good, and he had snagged several trout over twenty inches, including a beautiful eighteen-inch brown trout that he hated to throw back.

That night at the Sportsman's Lounge, after several beers and some tokes, a mysterious man, Jaime, began talking to Thunder Hawk. They hit it off and before the night was over, Thunder Hawk agreed to help him with a "delivery." They both knew what that meant. Daniel needed the money. Five months later, and several deliveries since, Thunder Hawk had become a full-fledged drug transporter.

After he proved himself, Jaime introduced Thunder Hawk to his boss, Luis *"El Tiburón"* Beltran – the Shark. He did not know much about *El Tiburón*. But he knew that it was his ticket to a lot of money. Things were looking up, way up.

Thunder Hawk rolled down the road, getting close to Crystal, north of Window Rock. This was the same beautiful mountain terrain that he had hunted and slept in. He let himself relax. A proud eagle soared through the endless blue sky. He reached down to switch the station on his radio.

"Nice! AC/DC," Thunder Hawk muttered.

He started singing along to "You shook me all night long" as he turned the volume up. His hand hit the steering wheel in rhythm to the music.

If only he had looked up a few seconds earlier, everything would have been different. When he looked back up at the road, it was too late.

Deer!

He screamed the word in his head. The doe and her fawns walked lazily across the road, unaware of their fast-approaching deaths. His reflexes and adrenaline were in overdrive. He turned the steering wheel hard right, but it was too late. His bumper slammed hard into the back of the startled doe, which tried to jump away but just couldn't make it. The deer crumpled and fell in the road as the fawns bounded away. Then, as if in a dream, Thunder Hawk flipped, over and over and over for what seemed like an eternity. His head crashed hard into the windshield, and then the world went black.

Officer Roland Begay had been in the Navajo Nation Police ten years. He rose in the ranks from "beat cop" to head of narcotics. The narcotics position was one of trust and influence. As his sphere of influence grew wider, his contacts within the drug world increased.

Pay wasn't so great in the police department, and the allure of drug money had been too much. Begay had an ex-wife, child to support, and an unfortunate gambling habit, which left him with too many debts.

The cartel stepped in and snagged Begay two years before. Jaime, the drug dealer from Farmington, made the arrangement, and the payments started coming pretty regularly. Five-thousand per month at first, increased to seven-thousand, and then ten-thousand per month. Begay's job was simple. He had to get the drug couriers safely through the Navajo Nation with the product. Begay had not had any problems until today.

The cartel told Begay to watch for Thunder Hawk to come through Crystal about this time. He was on his way over to check on him, to make sure that he made it to Sheep Springs on the reservation, but this wasn't how Begay expected to find Thunder Hawk.

The scene looked like a fatality; the wreck had just happened and the dust was still settling. As he rolled to a stop, Begay called dispatch for backup and requested air transport, in the event that Thunder Hawk had survived.

This is a bad one.

The wreckage was intense. Shattered glass lay strung out all over the side of the roadway. The Explorer had caved in on one side. A Coke can and papers were strewn all over the place. Begay looked closely to make sure that none of the "product" had leaked out. He tried to process how he would have the car towed for Thunder Hawk, before any of the first responders noticed anything was amiss.

Begay looked in front of the car and saw a deer in the road. The deer raised its head and tried to get up. It couldn't do it.

Its legs and back were probably broken.

There was nothing that could be done. Begay walked ahead a few steps, raised his sidearm and fired.

The deer jumped a bit and then slumped, out of its misery. Begay muttered a prayer.

Then he turned and walked towards the front of the car.

"Ahh," Thunder Hawk groaned and gasped.

Thunder Hawk lay to his right and his body writhed back and forth on the ground. Blood pooled beneath him.

"*Oh Lord.*" Begay said to himself.

Blood oozed thickly from Thunder Hawk's head. His left arm was visibly broken, and he was struggling to breathe. Begay ran to him.

Begay shouted into his phone, "This is Officer Begay! I need air rescue right now! I have serious injuries on scene!"

Thunder Hawk was grabbing his forehead and gasping for air. "My head, my head," while screaming in pain.

5

He breathed hard again and was trying to say something else. From his training Begay knew that Thunder Hawk had a serious head injury and was possibly bleeding inside his brain.

Begay leaned forward and touched Thunder Hawk's neck to feel for a pulse. He examined his eyes closely.

"I need air support! I have serious head injuries here!" Begay barked into his phone.

Thunder Hawk rolled towards him.

"Shit." Begay involuntarily uttered.

"Packages, where is … coke?" Thunder Hawk spoke in a guttural, almost whisper, as he recognized Officer Begay's voice.

Thunder Hawk and Begay both knew they were working with "them", and that if a problem happened on the reservation, he knew to call Begay.

Begay patted Thunder Hawk on the arm and whispered to him that it was okay. He looked over at the smashed Explorer as he gently pressed a cloth to Thunder Hawk's gaping head wound. He was barely conscious. Begay pressed two fingers to his neck. His pulse still felt pretty strong.

"Hang on, Daniel!" Begay shouted. "You are going to be ok! Hang in there." He screamed to anyone who was listening, "Where the hell is the medic?"

A siren sounded. Thunder Hawk coughed and gasped. Begay knew that he didn't have much time. The rag was soaked through with blood from the head wound and he was struggling to breathe. Begay again looked over at the Explorer, not seeing any drugs around it.

The sound of tires screeching interrupted his thoughts. As he looked over, a police cruiser pulled to a stop. When the door opened, former United States Marine Sergeant and now Navajo Nation Criminal Investigator, Joe Eagle, jumped out.

Joe was a member of the Navajo Nation and the proud grandson of one of the last surviving Navajo code talkers. He cut the classic figure of a Marine with a handsome chiseled face, dark hair and stern features. As an investigator, he was the best that the Navajo Nation had. Joe had grown up in the Navajo Nation, knew the terrain and people, and except for a year stint in Afghanistan with a Marine Recon unit, he had lived here his whole life.

During his tour in Afghanistan, Joe and his unit were assigned the dangerous job of hunting for Improvised Explosive Devises (IEDs) and detonating them before they could harm the troops. Only once had they missed finding an IED; Joe's instincts had been very, very good in locating them. But that one time still haunted him. The bomb had exploded, just as he was talking to one of his men inside their vehicle. It was deafening. Two men on Joe's team died, including the man next to him. Shrapnel hit Joe in his upper arm and neck, just below his jaw line. The Marines gave him a Purple Heart, which he did not feel he deserved. While the physical wounds had faded, the psychological wounds had not.

"Are you alright, Begay?" Joe shouted.

"I'm fine. But we don't have much time."

"Oh shit, he's bad."

Joe dropped to one knee and helped Begay apply pressure to the wound. Thunder Hawk was trying to speak, raspy and barely audible. He groaned and tried to raise his head.

"Easy, Daniel. Easy."

Begay put his hand on Thunder Hawk's shoulder. He continued applying pressure to the oozing head wound.

"His only hope is air rescue," Begay said.

Joe nodded. He had seen catastrophic injury and death in combat. They continued to press the cloth on Thunder Hawk's head wound.

After what seemed like forever, both heard the familiar chop chop chop of a helicopter. The aircraft came in fast, hovered, and set down about a hundred yards from the crash scene.

Dirt and dust whipped up from under the chopper. Medical personnel threw the door open, jumped out, and ran towards Begay and the group holding a "scoop" to carry Thunder Hawk to the chopper.

Thunder Hawk opened an eye and tried to speak as they lifted him onto the scoop.

Begay looked quickly at Joe. He changed his expression as Thunder Hawk muttered again about drugs and his car and Luis. Begay touched him gently to quiet him. He shot another glance towards the Explorer and then to Joe.

The paramedics were lifting Thunder Hawk gently and strapping him into the scoop. He moaned. He was now mumbling quietly about drugs and Jaime and Luis, not making any sense.

He is delusional from the lack of blood, Joe thought.

"Let's go! Go."

The paramedics were walking rapidly towards the helicopter holding Thunder Hawk as blood seeped onto the board underneath him.

The helicopter lifted and flew away, Begay walked over to the Explorer. Joe followed. More police units arrived on scene. Begay stepped forward just as Joe Eagle leaned towards the ground on the opposite side of the Explorer.

"Well looky here, boys. Looks like the driver was carrying more than beef jerky."

Joe looked up at Begay, who tried to turn away. The color was draining from his face.

Joe picked up the tightly wrapped package, torn in the middle. He moved the packaging aside. Inside was a white powdery substance that he had seen before - cocaine.

Begay leaned over and stared at two more packages on the ground. He started to walk away from the Explorer, looking back a few times. Other officers were coming over with their cameras to take pictures and "process" the scene.

Begay turned, and looked underneath the Explorer. It was propped up on one side on a rock. The engine block was broken, and there were other packages visible inside a not-so-secret compartment underneath the Explorer.

Begay walked farther away and opened his cell phone. He punched numbers into it. Joe could see that his face showed stress and concern.

Although Joe could not hear, Begay's call was to Luis "*El Tiburón*" Beltran.

El Tiburón worked for a Mexican cartel. No one really knew where he came from originally. Everyone said that his eyes were soulless. There was just nothing there.

He smuggled people and drugs for money. He liked the trade in people the best. Drugs were far more dangerous. The American authorities had declared war on them a long time ago.

New technology at the border and in the air was making it harder to make a living smuggling drugs. The Americans were more concerned with stopping drugs from crossing the border than they were with keeping illegal aliens out.

Of course, that didn't bother *El Tiburón*. In fact, he welcomed it. In the land of the blind, the one-eyed mouse was king. Not as many smugglers dealt in human cargo, which *El Tiburón* had always thought was odd.

While many people he knew had gone to American jails for smuggling drugs, few had gone to jail for smuggling people. Sure, every year some of the illegals would die in the blazing New Mexico sun from dehydration. But no one did much or tried to trace them back. They were just "illegals", and no one in the States really cared.

El Tiburón had ruthlessly taken over the people-smuggling business in Juarez, a victim at a time. One time he drowned a fellow smuggler in the Rio Grande after a night of hard drinking. After hitting several bars, El Tiburón suggested they take a walk to talk business. After a few minutes of chit chat, and after the man was completely relaxed, he waited for the right moment, turned to the side, and then turned back again in one violent motion, plunging a knife into the side of his new friend's neck. The man's eyes rolled back in his head. He ripped the knife downward in one quick, deadly efficient blow. Blood spurted everywhere.

The man jerked with shock, grabbed his neck, and plunged into the Rio Grande, sinking into its darkness. The water stained red for a moment, and then the current washed it clean again. Right up until the moment that the knife penetrated his neck, the other man thought that *El Tiburón* was his friend.

El Tiburón looked down at his phone as he stood in a plaza in Juarez, Mexico, and saw that it was the Navajo police officer calling.

"Hello."

"Luis, we have a problem."

"What is it?"

"Your guy from the reservation, Thunder Hawk was in a car accident. It rolled. These other officers, they just found it
in the car; and he was talking, Thunder Hawk was talking."

El Tiburón didn't have to ask what "it" was.

"Talking to who?"

"Officers and paramedics. It's not good. Your name was mentioned. And drugs." Begay was speaking as softly as he could. "They took him to Gallup Indian Medical Center. We have a serious problem."

"Is he going to live?"

"I don't know."

"Thanks. No need to call again."

El Tiburón abruptly hung up the phone, as Begay turned to look back at the crash scene.

As he looked, Begay noticed that the officers were stacking packages of cocaine on the back of a police cruiser. Some officers were dusting the inside of the Explorer for prints and collecting papers from inside. Another officer was walking a drug dog back to his car. This wasn't good. Begay involuntarily shuddered as his eyes locked with Joe Eagle's.

In Juarez, *El Tiburón* was calling a cartel member in Farmington, New Mexico.

CHAPTER 2

Joe made some notes onto a pad about what he had seen. His phone was ringing--Joe's grandmother. He answered.

"Grandma, how are you?"

"Not good, grandson. Please come right away."

"Are you ok?"

"I'm fine, but just come."

Joe hung up, headed outside, and jumped into his truck. Something big was happening. He could feel it, and had been unsettled for quite a while. He just couldn't put his finger on it. He hadn't slept well for weeks, and the nightmares were intense.

Joe thought a lot of it was related to his PTSD, but he tried to suppress that thought. He never considered himself 'weak' and felt like it would go away in time.

As he drove toward his grandmother's house, he was still thinking about the words of the medicine man from the night before. The medicine man repeated what the FBI had been saying. Drugs were coming into the reservation and the threat of danger was here. The words haunted him. It was an unknown danger, but Joe intuitively felt it. Joe wracked his brain for clues that he was missing.

How much danger are my people in? What is the danger? Who is responsible?

He had done the same mental exercise in Afghanistan. And he constantly reminded himself of one time, he had been wrong. He was stressed at the moment

12

and couldn't shake the thought that he was on the wrong path. He was missing something.

As Joe neared his grandmother's house, he saw police cars in and around the road in front. His grandmother was standing outside. Officers were talking to her.

Was she crying?

Joe's breathing accelerated, and the darkness swept into his head again. He flashed back to the time that his bomb detection group missed the IED in Afghanistan. It had been his third week on the job. Joe still believed it was his fault. They put him on administrative leave for a week and told him to "see a shrink." After a few visits, Joe lied and told the counselor that he had come to grips with what had happened.

The psychiatrist diagnosed him with PTSD, but that never went anywhere. She encouraged Joe to pursue a medical marijuana card and continue treatment. He politely declined. Instead, Joe spent nights trying to convince himself through quiet meditation that he could not have done anything different to change things.

It hadn't really worked, so he dealt with things in his own way.

Joe reached over and opened his console. He grabbed a miniature Jack Daniel's whiskey from inside. He twisted the cap and opened the bottle. So that no one could see, he leaned down and tipped the bottle and let the entire shot pour down his throat. It burned on the way down. Joe put the cap back on, hid the bottle back in the console and then got out of the car.

Shards of broken glass littered the road in front of his grandmother's house. A deep cut in the road ended abruptly in what looked like a terrible collision. They had towed the cars, but the metal and glass carnage told the story. Joe instantly knew this was bad.

I hope that this doesn't involve anyone I know.

As the alcohol began to relax him, he pushed his mind into that same meditative state. Joe got out and approached his grandmother. He was trying to breathe slowly.

"Grandma, what happened?"

"Hi *Shichai*," she smiled warmly, using the Navajo word for grandson. "Thank you for coming so quickly." She wrapped her arms around Joe's neck, and he returned the embrace. "Are you ok?"

"I'm ok. It was a bad car accident, right out in front. I heard it was awful.   I think they said the driver was drunk or on drugs. They took him to jail. The other one," she paused, "that young man did not make it."

She now started to sob, quietly at first.

Joe brought her in close to hug her.

Moments like this could trigger a deep primal rage in Joe and that scared him. It came from a part he couldn't see, deep inside, and once it arose; it was hard for Joe to put it down.

He thought back to his youth on the reservation. His dad, who had been a raging alcoholic, would sometimes beat his mom.

Joe intervened once, when he was eleven, and his dad turned on him, beating Joe until he blacked out. His mom tried to stop it. His father punished her with crushing fists.

When Joe finally awoke, his grandmother was holding him tightly in her arms. It was a safe place where he would remain, in a sense, until he graduated from high school. He lost his mom that night, and his dad, in a different way. Joe never went to the jail to visit his dad, and he doubted that he ever would.

Just then one of the officers who had been talking with his grandmother walked over to Joe.

"Hey, are you alright? Crazy day huh? First the guy rolls his car and dumps cocaine all over the place and now a fatal. Looks like alcohol. The drunk guy walked away again."

Joe shook his head.

"Oh by the way, I found an envelope with a piece of paper at that last scene with the cocaine guy. Looked odd. Thought you might make more sense out of it than me."

Joe grabbed the envelope. "Thanks. I appreciate it."

Joe glanced at the outside of the envelope.

Strange.

It had some kind of foreign writing, maybe Arabic or Hebrew. He paused for a moment in thought and pocketed the paper. Joe shook the officer's hand and said goodbye to his grandmother.

"Thank you again, grandson. Are you coming for dinner tonight?"

"I think that could be arranged." Joe smiled broadly, and his grandmother smiled back.

"I have to go, grandmother. I will see you tonight, ok? Be here about six."

"That's fine. See you then."

As Joe walked to his car, he pulled the paper out of his pocket and opened it. Again, there was a sentence of what looked like Arabic or some other Middle Eastern language. That's odd, Joe thought.

I'm going to have to look at this closer back at the office.

15

Later that night, the Eagle family and clan members hosted a feast with a traditional cleansing ceremony. It had been six months since Afghanistan. The medicine man summoned Joe and told him it was time to heal.

The medicine man cleansed Joe in an "enemy way" ceremony. Joe knelt down.

The medicine man touched him on the shoulders and chanted to reverse the process of giving him "power animals," which had protected and guided him on his journey while he was in Afghanistan. Those power animals were no longer necessary. Joe's power animal was a wolf. When he was fighting, he became the wolf and disassociated with the combat. The wolf fought for him and through him. Now he was safe again, back in his home, near the land that he loved, and for which he felt such a strong connection.

As the medicine man chanted an ancient chant, passed down through centuries, Joe knelt in quiet silence. His family looked on. When the medicine man finished, Joe rose. The medicine man patted him on the shoulder. Joe felt a new lightness that he hadn't felt in a long, long time.

After the ceremony the Eagle family talked and ate all of the food that the family members had prepared. Joe's aunts and uncles and grandmother laughed, cried, and chatted about how glad they were that Joe was back, safe and sound.

Joe was silent most of the time. A few times he slipped away to another room. He took a couple sips of alcohol to calm his nerves. These kinds of scenes made Joe uneasy and anxious, but he was happy that his family had all come together.

Towards the end, the medicine man took Joe aside.

"Joe, you have served your country well and for that we are all proud. It is so good to see you back safe here with us."

He paused for a moment, then repeated his prior words to Joe, "Here, in our home, in our land, we confront a new enemy. The drug dealers have come in. They have said they are a cartel, they use our kids, and they poison our people. It is bad, Joe, and it is here to stay unless we do something. The government does nothing. Our youth need our leadership, Joe. They need direction and guidance. We need you to fight. As hard as you fought for the government overseas, you fight here, for us."

Joe nodded. "I can only do my best. I don't know how to help right now, but I will find the way."

He embraced the medicine man.

In hindsight, this moment would prove to be the most pivotal in Joe Eagle's life. Hours later, as he lay in his bed, the medicine man's words were beating in his head like one hundred drums. The moment was one of calm peace mixed with great conflict. A storm was brewing, and the medicine man could sense it. Joe could sense it. Unbeknownst to either of them, that storm would soon dominate Joe's world, and, in the end, the entire country.

It would alter the balance of everything.

Joe couldn't sleep. When he finally dozed off, the medicine man was warning him, and he was shaking, and a giant fireball engulfed the reservation.

CHAPTER 3

El Tiburón slammed the door behind him and walked toward his favorite watering spot in Juarez, Mexico. This was going to be a lucrative day.

Chapulin de Colorado was a bar where he could relax. It was hidden well enough so that people in his line of work could avoid prying eyes of strangers.

The bar had a sordid history in the drug world. Several snitches had met the end of their lives in the back of the bar. One countertop was still stained faintly red. In a particularly violent moment, a cartel hit man gave a suspected snitch several shots of Patron and then forcefully rammed his head into the countertop until he slumped over and rolled to the floor. Even the most hardened criminals in the bar had turned away at the sickening sight. It was rumored that an owner associated with the bar had somehow been responsible for the kidnapping and murder of women who had gone missing in Juarez.

This wasn't your average neighborhood bar.

Today *El Tiburón* was meeting a new load of Arabs. The price was thirty-thousand dollars a head. He had smuggled Arabs before. Someone different would always contact him, with a blocked number. He never met the people who arranged, and paid for the loads.

The *La Raza* gang always escorted the Arabs to the same location in Juarez. He speculated about why the Arabs wanted to go to the United States. But in the end, he didn't care as long as they paid.

El Tiburón had a secret that only a very few people knew. Other smugglers had been amazed that he always seemed to avoid capture. It was almost like he was untouchable, but he had something going for him that few others had.

Eight years earlier, the CIA had secretly recruited him to watch the border for drug and gun smuggling.

They had numerous assets in Mexico, but the Agency had learned that smugglers like him often had the best intelligence about cartel operations.

The CIA paid him a generous fee every month, through an untraceable wire transfer to a bank in Juarez; in return, he provided information about drug and gun smugglers.

He always laughed when he picked up his cash. He was making money from the terrorists and the CIA, and neither knew about the other.

Over time, *El Tiburón* turned in several of his rival smugglers to his handlers, picking them off one by one. Meanwhile, he continued his smuggling unabated. It was the perfect double-cross.

Right now, he was sipping tequila inside the Colorado bar. Don Julio, silver, salted rim, no lime.

Some of the regulars lined the bar stools. He puffed on a Honduran cigar and watched the smoke float up to the ceiling.

In his mind, El Tiburón was a visionary. His plan was to resettle Mexicans in the land that they used to own.

"*Aztlan*" – the Southwestern United States was their land. The *gringos* forced them out at the point of a gun.

El Tiburón believed he was no different than Che Guevara and Emiliano Zapata, revolutionaries who went against the grain for the good of their people. Fighters like him, but his fight would be subtle, smarter. He would be an instrument of change through other means. He would resettle the southwestern United States, one smuggling load at a time, and if some Arabs or Africans wanted to cause trouble up there, so be it.

Juarez was hot, but the bar was cool and dark. He ordered a *Carta Blanca* beer. He waited for Hector, the *La Raza* guy, to call him and let him know that they were here.

For some time, the cartels had used members of the gang to provide protection on the journey to the United States border from Brazil. The Arabs were usually from Somalia and Palestine, but also had come from Jordan, Iran and Saudi Arabia.

Recently, he had also smuggled some people from West Africa into the United States. They traveled first to Brazil, because there were no passport requirements. They entered Mexico, again with no passport requirements, and finally met the gang members who brought them to Juarez and Tijuana. It was a lucrative industry, and *El Tiburón* wasn't going to quit anytime soon.

He looked down at his phone. It was Hector.
"Hector, how are you?"
"Very good, good. We are here."
"How many?"
"Eight."
"Okay, see you soon."
He hung up, motioned to the bartender for his tab, and placed the money on the bar. He donned his cowboy

hat and sunglasses and stepped through the heavy wooden bar door, past security, and back into the bright sunlight.

Decked out in his favorite black button-up shirt, belt with large buckle, and jeans, El Tiburon stepped forward confidently. He preferred to work alone, even though it was more dangerous.

Over the past several years, there had been a blood bath in Juarez with warring cartels. He personally ended the lives of several "snitches" during this war. It just wasn't worth sharing information with anyone. He didn't have a problem working for the cartel. He did his job for them and they paid him, simple as that.

As he walked out, one of the two security guards made a comment under his breath in Spanish: "*Ahi va la muerte caminando*." (There goes death walking).

The doors shut and the guards went back inside.

El Tiburón pulled up to the *Chamizal Plaza*, about two miles from the United States' border. In the back were several small, nondescript houses. He pulled around to the back of the middle house and waited inside his car for approximately five minutes.

Seeing nothing out of the ordinary, he shut down his engine and walked toward the house at the end of the park. As he drew close he sent a short text:

Bien.

Moments later the back door swung open, and he hurried inside.

"The money's in the bank," Hector said as he came inside.

El Tiburón made a quick call and confirmed that all $240,000 had been transferred. The transfers made their way from accounts overseas, through various car dealerships in the United States, and ultimately to a bank in Costa Rica. A man in Lebanon set up this complex laundering scheme, which was funded by numerous unidentified investors. *El Tiburon* never had a problem because it was beyond difficult to trace, and he had friendly bankers in Costa Rica.

At midnight, Hector, *El Tiburón*, eight young Saudi and Jordanian men climbed into two sport utility vehicles that were parked about a block down the road from the houses. The men hid beneath the back seats.

The cartel drivers drove below the speed limit to avoid law enforcement scrutiny. They made it without incident to an area south of the international border, near Santa Teresa, New Mexico, to a tunnel close to where the trains crossed.

This tunnel stretched nearly three hundred yards underground from Mexico and ended in an open field near Santa Teresa. Workers spent months building it. It was painstaking and dangerous work. The men excavated and hammered the wooden frame into the earth at night. The tunnel's existence was a very closely guarded secret in the cartel. Recently, the border patrol had deployed robots to assist in finding tunnels, but this tunnel had not been located. It was a very effective thoroughfare by which *El Tiburón* moved drugs and people into the United States.

Hector and *El Tiburón* stopped their sport utility vehicles a mile away from where they needed to go, in a remote area in an alley. The owner of the home in Mexico where they parked was paid five thousand dollars per month to claim ownership of the vehicles if need be, but there had never been a problem.

The whole group dressed in black. They followed as *El Tiburón* began the trek to the safe house. His destination was a false door in the basement that opened to the entrance of the tunnel.

As they entered the house, *El Tiburón* walked to the trap door and opened it. He motioned for the men to step down into the basement. After each of the Saudis and Jordanians, all Jihadists, made it through the trap door and into the area below, Hector said goodbye and left. *El Tiburon* closed the trapdoor and flicked on a small flashlight. Seconds later, he opened the false door and the group, one by one, ducked inside the tunnel.

El Tiburón shut off the flashlight. Darkness enveloped them. As they were instructed, each man reached out and grabbed the belt of the person in front of him. They had to stoop slightly to avoid hitting the roof, which was a mere five feet tall, and lined with heavy wooden beams for support.

He walked slowly, leading them forward by the light of lanterns on the floor, as well as by his memory.

As they crept forward, dirt fell in small clumps and dusted them. There was little noise except the sounds of their footsteps. The men smelled a damp, musty odor. This tunnel was not a place where one would want to linger overnight.

Thirty minutes later, *El Tiburón* halted and turned on his phone for just long enough to send a text, and then he shut it down. Now, they were moving again. They walked for a short while and then stopped. Faint moonlight could now be seen through a tiny slit at the end of the tunnel. It was a welcome sight. The men's heart rates quickened in anticipation. Everyone stopped, knelt down, and waited for the signal to move.

Approximately one and a half miles away, two young agents with Homeland Security, and a newly-promoted Sergeant with the Georgia National Guard, watched for people trying to cross over from Mexico.

This area of New Mexico is dry desert land, with small trees and brush dotting the landscape. The night sky is usually full of stars, and visibility is almost always good. Tonight it was slightly cool, and there was a light breeze.

The agents worked well together in catching illegal crossers, and they expected tonight to be no different. As they watched their area of responsibility, they passed the time talking football, bureaucracy and good-looking southern girls. While they waited for some action, they glanced from time to time into their Forward Looking Infrared (FLIR) Unit.

A FLIR unit measures heat signals and is very accurate in detecting the movement of people. The unit can see through the dark and identify people who have no way of seeing the FLIR operator, unless they have night vision. Few border crossers had that kind of technology. On this night there was no moon, so the FLIR was even more important for visibility.

Unfortunately, they had the FLIR pointed in the opposite direction from where the tunnel exited into the United States.

After a short time talking, one of the agents spied a small group of people creeping slowly and carefully across the border from Mexico.

"Haha. Here we go. It's like shooting fish in a barrel boys."

"Where are they? Oh yea, I see them. Let's go get 'em."

In seconds, the three men were inside their government-issued Jeep and driving slowly, "lights out" toward the group of illegals. They switched on their night vision goggles. As they neared the illegal crossers, the agents shined their flashlights and rolled forward to a stop. Everything happened so quickly that the crossers had no chance to react. The agents jumped out and ran forward, training their flashlights on them. The illegals immediately dropped to the ground.

The lead agent shouted in Spanish.

"*¡Federales Americanos*! *¡Congelar! ¡Manos arriba!* (Homeland Security! Freeze! Hands Up!)*"

Without hesitation, all three men raised their hands and placed them on the back of their heads.

The agents moved forward, guns drawn, until they were above the crossers, and then, one by one, they handcuffed them. The Sergeant called for backup to transport the illegals to the Santa Teresa station. Backup arrived shortly, and the agents walked the crossers into the back of the patrol unit and headed for the station.

The agents spent a couple hours processing the illegal immigrants.

They ran them through the IDENT system to check for previous crossings, and then entered them into the Homeland Security databases for cross-referencing, to make sure the system would pick them up the next time they tried to cross the border and enter the United States.

Even though these particular individuals did not appear to be dangerous, it was a priority to document everyone for the next time they might try to come in.

The agents finished processing the immigrants for removal proceedings in El Paso.

Later that night, after the immigrants were put on a bus for the Texas border, and then to Mexico, the agents slapped hands, congratulating themselves for their great work. If they continued their streak of consecutive nights of successfully busting people, they would all be up for promotion. In the process of accumulating a few stats with these arrests, and enjoying their love fest, the agents missed what could have been the biggest bust of their careers.

At the very moment the three illegals were being led away and arrested, *El Tiburón* received the text back:

Bien.

He waited a short time and then he opened the double trap doors. He punched a button on his scanning device, and a miniature mirror rose up and projected through the trap door and out into the outside. The device was attached to a computer, on the screen *El Tiburón* could see what the miniature camera could see. He turned it all directions.

Seeing no danger, he lowered the camera. He poked his head out, and not seeing anyone, he climbed out.

As he scanned the horizon, each of the Jihadists now began to emerge, ever so slowly, from the tunnel. When the last one exited, they began crawling over thorns and rocks in a line through the New Mexico desert.

After about fifty feet, they reached the pickup point, which was in natural cover behind a bluff. They lay there for several minutes. They saw movement in the distance, and another man appeared. The man waved, and *El Tiburón* rose up onto his knee.

He motioned for the group to follow him.

The man, a member of *La Raza*, and the group of Jihadists walked in a crouch position to the north. When they got to a van, hidden behind a group of trees, *El Tiburón* shook the *La Raza* man's hand. The Jihadists jumped into the van and sped off into the night.

And with that, *El Tiburón* again handed the load – this time Arabs - over to his gang contact. They had successfully entered the United States again, and, for whatever reason, *El Tiburón* didn't care. His money was fully earned.

"Stupid Americans. How easy is this?"

As he always did, he turned around, and hurriedly ran back to the tunnel. He shot one more glance back into the night sky. It was beautiful. The stars shone brightly. As he closed and locked the trap doors, behind him, and he was safe inside the tunnel again, he slipped a tequila pint from his pocket. Patron Silver; only the best. He took a swig and began the trek back to Mexico.

CHAPTER 4

The safe house was a three-bedroom, one-story dwelling with brown stucco. Someone had pulled the shades closed. The house had a one-car garage and the typical xeriscape yard. A trashcan sat at the top of the driveway. There was nothing about the house that set it apart from any of the other ones in the neighborhood. But this house was not what it seemed. It now housed multiple Jihadists who were in the United States on a mission.

After holing up for the night and the next day in the safe house, the Jihadists began to grow antsy. They waited for their moment to leave, so they could reunite with their brethren.

The leader, Agha, surveyed the group of warriors with him. They were all expertly trained men. All were loyal to a fault and eager to accomplish the mission ahead of them.

Agha had recently turned forty. With silver streaks cutting through his dark hair and deepening lines running through his forehead, Agha cut the profile of a man who had experienced much hardship and death, which he had.

He grew up in war-torn Afghanistan.

His family migrated there from Iran. Iranian authorities sent his dad to join the fight against the Americans and the Russians. Agha did not know why they were there; he just knew that he was always scared when the bombs would start.

He was always very close to his mom. Oftentimes, he would walk outside his house holding her hand. She would gently pat his head. His friends would tease him for this behavior. He didn't care though, because it made him feel safe.

And then one fateful and tragic day, Agha went outside to kick a ball around with a friend. They played for a little while, occasionally staring across the field at a couple of young girls who were talking. Were they staring at them? Agha tried a few "trick" kicks to get their attention.

Suddenly, people were screaming and running and yelling for everyone to run and take cover! Agha and his friend froze. They looked at the people who were scattering. The girls were running.

What was going on?

Then, Agha and his friend started running.

They sprinted into a nearby abandoned building and took cover inside a small room, which had a window that looked out into the field.

Agha raised his head over the window-sill and saw his dad.

"Dad!" Agha yelled out.

He was running across that field towards their house. Agha thought he was running to get him. Events seemed to move in slow motion. His dad was trying to run, and Agha was yelling and shouting for him.

As Agha stood in the window and held his arms up waving, an explosion rocked him. BOOM!!

Agha ducked and hit the floor hard. His friend hit the floor also.

When Agha got back up a few moments later, he looked out into the field but his dad was gone.

Nothing.

Agha ran out into the field, over his friend's screams to stop. He looked everywhere.

Nothing. Emptiness.

After a time his mom came to pick him up. Agha was lying there in the field clutching a small piece of shrapnel to his chest. His mom pleaded with him. He finally stood up. He cried that day and for days after. The loneliness was intense.

Neither Agha nor his mom or brother ever found any of the dad's remains. They never saw him again. He just vanished in a moment of time. They later learned that a missile fired from an American fighter plane had wiped out forty-nine people in one fell swoop. It changed Agha's life.

He broke down for several weeks.

One day Agha abruptly stopped crying. He fixed his jaw and became a man, seemingly overnight. He left the house, and at age twelve, he took up the fight on his own. His mom tried to stop him but to no avail. He believed that his father would live on through him.

Just a child, but with an excellent aptitude for weapons and fighting, Agha took to the streets and began shooting the enemy. It wasn't long before others noticed, and they taught him how to shoot as a sniper. He became one of the best snipers in his village and surrounding areas. He relished seeing one of his enemies in his scope, right before he would pull the trigger, knowing that he literally held life and death in his hands at that moment. He always chose death. Because for each one he killed, it was one that couldn't kill someone else's father or brother.

On this day, his mission was no less important. The men in Iran had appointed him for this most important of missions after he successfully bombed a train in Italy. He was perhaps the most accomplished at his trade and elusive as a fox. His eyes, dark and foreboding, reflected sheer determination.

Agha sensed chaos and danger and believed that the time was drawing nigh to unleash the terror he had planned. He decided they would unleash it all sooner than expected. This mission must be accomplished at any cost.

Makeshift beds and sleeping bags littered the interior of the house. Uneaten green chili and meat burritos sat on the kitchen counter. Everyone was quiet.

The *La Raza* guards who maintained the house had been making calls throughout the day.

Finally, at 9:30 p.m., they signaled it was time to go. The plan was to time the passage through the border patrol checkpoint on Interstate 25 near Las Cruces, New Mexico, when there was a planned shift change for the agents. At that moment, the agents would not be as attentive to cars coming through, and the men had the best chance of passing through without detection or incident.

The *La Raza* driver ushered the group out of the house and into the dark SUV. This particular vehicle had been meticulously cleaned and swept of any drug leaves or residue. It had been scrubbed until it was pristine and then scrubbed again. Another *La Raza* member rode in the passenger seat. Their driver's licenses were clean with no criminal history, and the plates on the SUV were as well. A contact in the Department of Motor Vehicles had checked to make sure that there were no problems that would show up on a computer check.

The gang had carefully handpicked the two *La Raza* members to transport this most important cargo. They had no visible tattoos and could speak perfect English. They were drilled for weeks on how to answer specific questions and how to react to specific situations. There was no room for error. The orders were simple:

Failure is not an option. Even if you have to shoot to kill, get the Arabs to the destination point, period.

They shoved their loaded mini Glock .32 caliber pistols beneath their seats.

Meanwhile, Agha and his Jihadists were climbing into false compartments built into the footrests of the back two layers of seats. Although uncomfortable, it was their best chance to pass through the checkpoint. *La Raza* told them that the next forty-five minutes would be the most dangerous of the trip, and they weren't to move or say anything.

The Jihadists recited silent prayers that Allah would be with them.

And then they were moving. The driver pulled onto Interstate 25 north at the University exit and set the cruise control for sixty-five miles per hour. Everyone's nerves were on edge. The Arabs rode silently in their hiding places.

Approximately thirty minutes north, the border patrol agents were completing their shift change at the I-25 checkpoint. Northbound, coming from Las Cruces, cars were being directed by a series of orange cones, and declining speed limit signs, into one of two large "carport" structures. Before they stopped inside the open-air carports, the cars would go through a line of cameras, which photographed every license plate. Next to the carports were small trailers where the agents could interrogate suspects and take a break from 'the line'. On almost every shift, at least one K-9 unit, or drug detecting dog and his handler were present.

This checkpoint on I-25 represented the last line of defense to intercept drug and immigrant smuggling. Once someone made it through this checkpoint, there was a small, manned border patrol station at Truth or Consequences, but there were no further checkpoints to get through.

At the checkpoint, the agents were performing their shift change an hour earlier than usual, which they did on occasion to throw off drug smugglers who tried to time the shifts.

A supervisor announced earlier in the day during routine briefing to expect a marijuana shipment to come through the checkpoint. An anonymous tipster had called into the hotline.

In reality, *La Raza* had arranged the marijuana shipment. It was a decoy load, designed to go through the checkpoint fifteen minutes before the "actual" load of Arabs, which would pass through without incident once the agents were occupied taking apart the decoy car.

The fall guy, a young *La Raza* member named Paco, volunteered to drive the decoy load.

He drove a 1980s Mustang, with different tags to make the car appear to be stolen. *La Raza* loaded it with enough marijuana to make the feds interested, but not enough to secure him a long sentence. *They* would pay him generously for his efforts.

Senior gang members coached him to show signs of nervousness; make nonsensical statements and fumble his driver's license when asked to produce it. Once the agents questioned him, he was to break down and confess.

Paco's gang leaders told him that he would have only limited time to make this arrest go down. He was not told about the load of Arabs that would be following him within minutes through the checkpoint.

It all would have worked like a charm had the Mustang's tire not blown less than a mile before the checkpoint. He felt the car shudder slightly, and then it lurched hard to the left, setting down low on the left side. Sparks flew as metal hit road, and it was all Paco could do to get the Mustang over to the side. The car ground to a sickening halt.

"Shit! Shit!"

Paco opened his door and jumped out. The rear driver's side tire was ripped to shreds.

"Dammit! No. No!"

Paco knew that he had no time to change the tire before he was supposed to drive through the checkpoint. Beads of sweat rolled down his forehead. Paco panicked. He had been told not to fail, or else. He opened his cell phone and called his boss.

"The tire, the tire … it's blown …!"

"Slow down! What? What happened? What Paco?!"

"My tire, it blew. I can't fix it; I can't fix it in time."

"Where are you?"

"Almost at the checkpoint. I can see it …"

The phone went dead.

Seldom do plans go exactly as they should. When the driver of the Jihadists hit ten minutes out from the checkpoint, he turned off his cell phone, as he'd been instructed. He was almost there. At the same time, Paco's boss was calling over and over to the now silenced cell phone to warn him, but to no avail.

A border patrol agent looked out from the checkpoint and saw the stalled car. Thinking someone might need help, he got in his patrol car and drove southbound on Interstate 25 and did a U-turn at the nearest official– use-only-crossover.

As he pulled back onto I-25 North, he pulled in behind a dark SUV. He accelerated to sixty-five miles per hour, and in a short time, saw the stopped car. He engaged his emergency equipment and pulled in behind the Mustang.

Before he did so, the *La Raza* driver saw the border patrol agent perform the U-turn and pull in behind him. Adrenaline surged, and his heart felt as though it were beating through his chest wall. His calm exterior turned into panic. He looked at his passenger who reached underneath his seat to grab his Glock.

As they neared the checkpoint, beads of sweat began to run down the driver's face. He looked uneasily back and forth at his fellow gang member, and at the rear view mirror.

When the border patrol agent engaged his emergency lights, the driver thought they had been caught. He floored the accelerator at the moment the speed limit reduced to enter the checkpoint.

As the driver hit eighty-five in a forty-five zone, he looked in the rear view mirror and saw the Mustang pulled over, and the agent rolling in behind it. The *La Raza* driver braked hard to get down to the thirty-five limit.

"Shit."

The gang member in the passenger seat placed the Glock under his leg. The driver breathed hard and tried to control his emotions. He slowed and pulled in behind a car being questioned by an agent. They were next. The agent waived the car ahead and motioned the SUV to enter the inspection area.

Border Patrol Agent Thompson, was checking other vehicles moments ago when he saw this particular SUV accelerate, and then brake hard as it was nearing the checkpoint. It caught his eye because of the agent's flashing lights.

Very suspicious.

The SUV stopped in front of him.

"Good evening gentlemen. Everyone a U.S. Citizen?"

"Um, yes, yes sir," the driver and passenger responded in unison.

Agent Thompson thought he caught a hint of nervousness. Something was off.

"Can I see your license and registration?"

"Sure, Officer. Sure thing."

The driver fumbled a bit as he was taking out his license to show the Agent. He handed it over.

Thompson glanced at the license and looked back up at the driver.

"Wait here for a minute."

As Thompson walked away, the driver's mind was screaming *go, go, go.*

The passenger had put his hand on his gun. Below, the Arabs sensed that something was wrong. One of them moved, and the driver glanced nervously to the back.

The driver looked up. Thompson was peering into the back of the SUV through the rear window.

"Oh shit."

More beads of sweat. The driver didn't know what to do, and he was beginning to panic. Thompson turned and walked into a building.

The driver's instincts told him to floor it. He looked at the passenger and switched the gear into drive. The passenger tensed. Seconds before the driver gunned it to escape, another agent walked in front of the SUV with his drug detection dog, Luka. Then another agent appeared on the passenger side and ducked down. He was holding some kind of mirror. The driver changed the gear back into park.

Luka and the agent circled the exterior of the SUV. The other agent looked under it with the mirror. The driver and the passenger struggled hard to keep their composure. Although they had been trained to expect this, it was different when it was actually happening, and a drug dog was walking around the car.

At the moment of maximum peril, Thompson returned to the driver's side window. Luka and the agent had completed the round, and saw no sign of drugs. This was not the load car that the agents were looking for.

"Ok, sir. Your license checks out. Seems everything is fine. Have a good trip."

The driver nodded. He felt intense relief.

He pushed the accelerator, a little too hard at first, and then steadied it as they rolled out of the checkpoint. No one said a word.

The driver switched his phone back on. There were seventeen missed calls and ten texts. He handed the phone to his passenger, who texted back:

All clear.

On the other end of the text, the *La Raza* boss breathed a sigh of relief as he realized that he would live another day.

The SUV rolled ahead, without incident, past Truth or Consequences. As they hit Socorro, the driver took the route that the gang bosses had told him to take. They drove through several smaller roads, and, finally, over the Chuska Mountains, where Daniel Thunder Hawk had crashed, to their destination in Navajo, Arizona. All of these roads were essentially off grid so they would have little chance of being stopped.

As they pulled into Navajo, exhausted and on edge from the events of the night, the Jihadists finally emerged from their hiding place. The SUV rolled to a stop at a safe house on the Navajo Reservation. The driver exited first with the passenger, and they went inside. Shortly after, Agha and his group went inside.

As the eight men entered, they saw their other nine comrades for the first time in six months, and they all shouted
"Praise Allah! Praise Allah! Praise Allah!"

As they embraced, the driver stepped outside and sent a text to *El Tiburón*:

The package is delivered and safe.

El Tiburón's phone buzzed, and the words that he was waiting to hear appeared on the screen. He shut off his phone, walked outside and got into his car. He drove to the Internet Café closest to his home in Juarez. When he got inside he signed in with his password and pseudonym into the "deep web."

The "deep web" was largely still a secret to the general public, but was used extensively by drug smugglers and others engaged in criminal schemes. Estimates posted on Google were that over ninety percent of the available data and information on the "web" was actually inside the "deep web." Google and other basic search engines held a small percentage of the available data by contrast.

After passing through some encrypted addresses, the message reached a very powerful man in the cartel in Mexico City. A loyal employee of the cartel boss walked to an internet café in Mexico City and sent another encrypted message to a man in Iran.

At an internet café on Valiasr Street in Tehran, Iran, a man signed into the internet and received the message:

Judgment day is nigh.

He smiled and signed off. A few blocks walk away he stepped inside the house of his loyal friend and partner, Ahmed. They poured some tea.

He boasted, "We will kill three hundred thousand Americans. They will hear our voice again on their own shores. We will not wait for Israel to harm us. We will act first. *InSha 'Allah*."

CHAPTER 5

Meanwhile, Joe had the envelope open on his desk and the contents, a one-page note, in front of him. Using some software that the federal government had recently provided to the Navajo Nation through a grant, he scanned the cryptic Arabic message into a program, which read and translated the text:.

الوقت يقترب. تبقى قوية. وسيتم إعلامك قريبا.'

The translation program immediately displayed its English meaning:

The time is drawing close. Stay strong. You will be notified soon.

This isn't good.
Joe closed his computer. He got up to leave the office and head outside.
Joe reflected on what his FBI contact, Agent Maria Spencer had recently told him. Arabs were thought to be hiding in the Navajo Nation or on Hopi land. They have not been able to locate them.
Now he was alarmed. There had to be some connection between the drugs and Arabs. And it looked like something was going to happen soon.
Daniel Thunder Hawk would have more answers.
Joe decided that he would go see him. The drugs were tied to the Arabs. This note came from Thunder

Hawk's car. He must be delivering drugs-- and a message.

Now I just have to figure out to who and why.

Joe walked outside the criminal investigation office in Fort Defiance and called the hospital, and the Navajo Housing Authority.

His contact at the hospital said that Thunder Hawk had undergone fairly extensive treatment but was recovering remarkably. The hospital had recently released him, and he was at his house.

Grabbing the envelope and the note, Joe jumped into his unmarked police cruiser, an older model Dodge Durango.

He drove for about an hour before he got to the Navajo Housing Authority in Newcome. He found Thunder Hawk's house pretty quickly. He walked up to the door and knocked.

"Hold on, be right there."

Seconds later, the door opened. A young man with long dark hair and a bandaged head stepped outside.

Definitely him.

"Can I help you?" Thunder Hawk nervously paced back and forth.

"Daniel Thunder Hawk?"

"Yes, that's me."

Joe extended his hand. "My name is Joe Eagle with criminal investigations. I'm not here to arrest you. I want to ask you some questions, if you wouldn't mind, about your crash and some other matters."

Thunder Hawk looked down and shuffled his feet. He looked up again and nodded. Thunder Hawk turned and waved Joe inside the house.

"Do I need my lawyer? I mean, I don't want any more trouble than I already have."

"That's totally up to you. I need some information about what's going on at the reservation. It could be important for our people. I just want to find out about the drugs and this." Joe held the envelope with the Arabic writing out in front of Thunder Hawk.

Thunder Hawk swallowed hard and the color drained from his face.

He stuttered. "Where ... where did you find that?"

"It was in your car, Daniel. It has your fingerprints on it." Joe was bluffing. The gambit worked.

Thunder Hawk now shook slightly. "Yes, umm, the man at the border gave it to me. I was supposed to deliver it to another guy in Farmington."

"What are their names?" Joe asked.

Thunder Hawk paused. "You aren't recording this are you?"

"No. We want this information, but your name won't be used."

Thunder Hawk nodded his head and continued. "These guys are dangerous, Mr. Eagle. I told the FBI, so I guess there's no harm in telling you also." He looked at Joe's face for clues as to whether he could trust him.

Joe stepped forward. "Daniel, you have my word. I need this information and it might save lives. I fear something awful is about to happen." Joe looked him right in the eyes.

Daniel Thunder Hawk rocked forward in his seat and nodded. "The man at the border is named *El*

Tiburón. He runs the cartel's drugs and smuggling. The man I see in Farmington is Jaime. Jaime Avelan. I run drugs for them, or at least I used to. I'm looking at a lot of time I think. Need to figure out a better path." Thunder Hawk looked down at the floor. "The envelope was from *El Tiburón*. It was supposed to go to Jaime. I heard that they smuggled some more Arabs in. They are somewhere near Navajo Village. I don't know what they are here to do. I know they run a lot of drugs."

Joe nodded his head while taking notes. He asked a few more questions about routes and how long Thunder Hawk had been smuggling, how much he was paid, and contacts. Thunder Hawk was also able to produce one more important piece of information. It seemed that the cartel was rumored to use a tunnel at the border.

As they wrapped up, Joe leaned forward, shook Daniel's hand and placed his other hand on his shoulder. "There are better paths Daniel. I feel that you will find your way."

Joe patted his shoulder and walked outside to his car. As he pulled away, he saw Thunder Hawk standing in his doorway, watching.

Before he drove one hundred yards, Joe saw a Navajo Police car coming from the opposite direction, speeding towards him. He recognized Officer Begay as he pulled up to Thunder Hawk's house.

Damn. I think I know what this is about. How did he know I was here?

Joe made a mental note about his drive over, and went back over the events in his head, but could not remember any surveillance.

My phone?

Joe turned his car towards Navajo village. If Thunder Hawk was right, someone would alert the Arabs soon. Joe thought that he might be able to see some activity. In effect, he had just kicked the hornet's nest, and now it was time to watch them fly.

As he entered Navajo village, Joe pulled out a small map of various roads and houses that could possibly be a place to hide. He studied the map for a few minutes, trying to remember where he'd seen criminal activity in the past. He also looked for likely "safe houses" but could not pinpoint any house in particular. Joe decided to conduct some surveillance.

At the exact same time Joe was making his decision, two FBI Special Agents were speeding by Daniel Thunder Hawk's house, looking for Joe.

Joe eased his car down several dirt roads as he searched for the home or area that could be holding the Arabs. He looked from house to house, and all seemed pretty normal.

Seeing nothing unusual, he circled back to the village center. As he neared the center, he saw a black, very official looking car appear in his rear view mirror. The men in the car placed an emergency light on the top and lit it up. They motioned for Joe to pull over.

"Geez, here we go," Joe muttered to himself.

He pulled to a stop on the side of the road. He opened the driver's door and started to get out just as the men in the black car walked rapidly towards his passenger side.

"FBI! Keep your hands where we can see them!"

The FBI agent placed his right hand on his side arm and drew it.

"Whoa, whoa, easy. What's the problem?" Joe spoke calmly.

"The problem is you!" The agent was now yelling. "You're sniffing around where you don't belong! What's your authority here, Mr. Eagle?" Before Joe could answer the agent answered his own question. "None!"

The agent now lowered his firearm slightly.

"Agents, I am with Navajo Criminal Investigations. I have full authority to investigate matters within the Navajo Nation."

Joe was polite but firm. This was not his first run in with the FBI. In fact, any time there was a significant investigation on the reservation, Joe just waited for the FBI to arrive.

"Well Mr. Eagle, you don't have any authority in this investigation, and you are not to approach Daniel Thunder Hawk again unless we ask you to do so! If our supervisor needs to call yours, we will do that also. Are we clear?"

Joe took a step forward and then thought better and stopped his forward motion. "That's fine. You let me know when you need help."

Joe turned and walked back to his car.

The FBI agents' faces were smug as they hopped into their car and slammed the doors. They had made their point clear, and Joe would stay out of the way, or at least they thought so.

When the FBI agents stopped, they forgot to turn off the
emergency lights, which had now been flashing for a couple of minutes. The flash was enough to draw the attention of several of the residents. They watched from their porches as the FBI agents sped away.

In one home, a young Hispanic male was on the porch listening to the FBI agent's shouting. He watched intently and tried to identify any of the faces. He thought he recognized the cop from the reservation but wasn't sure. He ducked back into the house.

In a fairly recently dug and furnished basement below, seventeen Arabs sat motionless, waiting and listening.

The *La Raza* member popped his head into the staircase opening. He walked a few steps and signaled that there was trouble. He told Agha they would move tonight or the next night. This location was no longer safe.

Within the hour, the Arabs packed their small bags and prepared to leave. The *La Raza* member made a brief cryptic call to Jaime and let him know they had to move.

Jaime told him he would have the new location tomorrow, and would be there to move them. He then hung up and made another call to Officer Begay, who answered right away.

"What's the problem?"

"It's Thunder Hawk. He's talking. We had some visitors." Begay knew he shouldn't say much over the phone.

"Ok, well, we need to get rid of our problems. I'll take care of it." Jaime hung up and cursed.

He called *El Tiburón*, who said even less over the phone, only to move and move fast. *El Tiburon* didn't have to remind Jaime of the importance of protecting the Arabs. Jaime was already on the move when he hung up.

At his house, Daniel Thunder Hawk had a bad feeling that he couldn't shake. He sat down on the floor and prayed and meditated as he had done throughout his life when he felt the demons. He asked for wisdom and strength.

As he drifted off to sleep in his chair, his mind was anything but calm. It was active and troubled. The demons were circling. They were on the move, and he could feel them hunting him.

CHAPTER 6

Joe ordered a second Corona and a shot as he sat back in his chair and continued to think about what Thunder Hawk had said, the drug problems, and what it meant with the Arabs. He stared at the television over the "Tijuana bar", the main hangout these days near Sheep Springs. His favorite football team, the Dallas Cowboys, was losing another heartbreaker. It was almost too much to take.

Can that damn Romo quit going to beaches and dating hot chicks and just play football?

The main door opened and a young man walked in. He was one of Joe's informant, Ben, a twenty-two year old part-time musician and miscreant from the nearby Hopi reservation.

"Sorry I'm late."

"No problem at all, Ben. Glad you could make it."

He pulled a chair back and took a seat next to Joe. He ordered his usual, Jack Daniels and coke. Joe gestured at the TV screen and made a look of disgust as Ben laughed.

"Gotta root for the Raiders, Joe. I keep telling you. At least we know we aren't going to be good. See, you guys just always think this is the season, every year. I'm used to the disappointment."

Joe laughed hard. His nerves were so frayed these days that a meeting with Ben was a good idea, even if he had nothing to offer.

Joe took another drink and asked: "Ben what do you know about what's going on at Navajo Village.

"That's going to cost you," Ben laughed.

The waitress was back, as she usually was, within seconds of Ben sitting down.

"I'll have a Corona also."

Ben smiled from ear to ear, like he was the king of the place.

This was the one thing that constantly annoyed Joe about dealing with informants. They all had their individual quirks. Some were complete drunks. Some were druggies. Some were just flat out weird. Most of them had an extensive criminal history. You had to learn to work them and it took time. Informants were a dangerous group, because they were prone to exaggerating and making things up, as Joe had seen repeatedly. Ben had always been pretty straight up, save for his occasional jerkiness.

His problem was that he was arrogant and an unmitigated drunk, and someday, Joe thought, it would be his downfall.

Joe downed his shot.

"What about the FBI, Joe? Are they going to get into my shit? I've been hearing things. I heard they stopped you in Navajo."

"Screw the FBI!" Joe laughed and then ordered Ben a shot.

"Ben, don't worry about the FBI. We can deal with them."

"Yea, well, I don't think you got that much power bro. Know what I am saying? I don't want to go back to the joint is all." Ben continued, "Anyway, let me tell you what's up, Joe. There've been some things going on, like you said, in Navajo. People seeing some strange stuff. Yea, there is something about Arabs living there. I've seen them from time to time. But I don't think they will be there for long. The feds are running around and stopping people and shit. They'll be gone soon."

Joe was listening intently now. "Can you tell me where to look? Where are they?"

"I don't know, Joe. These guys, they move around a lot. They're like ghosts."

Ben ordered another shot, and Joe placed his half-finished beer on the table.

"Alright, thanks."

Joe placed thirty dollars on the table to cover the drinks.

"Hey, thanks, my brother. Good stuff. I'll be seeing you soon." Ben gestured with his full shot glass and Joe stood up to leave.

"As always Ben, it's been real. Keep your nose to the ground for me about these guys in Navajo, ok?"

"Sure."

Joe left the bar and headed over to see Eldon Tsosie, the medicine man, who'd texted him fifteen minutes earlier. When he got to the house, the medicine man ushered him into his living room. Pipe smoke lingered in the air. The television was on, and a program on the History channel was playing, something about World War II.

"Joe, thanks for coming. Have a seat. Do you want some coffee? Just made a batch a little bit ago."

The medicine man walked into the kitchen.

"Sure, thanks a lot."

"The reason why I asked you to come down is that I need some help from one of our brothers up north. For reasons you don't need to know right now, we've had several meetings recently on other matters. I'm talking about the Northern Cheyenne and their Dog Soldiers. Have you heard of them?"

The medicine man handed Joe a cup of coffee.

"No, I don't think so? Maybe I remember something vaguely. Aren't they all gone?"

The medicine man laughed.

"Not hardly, Joe. The Dog Soldiers date back hundreds of years, back to the time when settlers first came west across the northern plains. Their original purpose was to protect the tribe from raids by other nations and the Union army." The medicine man took a drink from his cup of coffee, as did Joe. "The Dog Soldier's purpose was to protect the tribe and he did so at all costs, which included the risk of his own death. The original ones had a braided rope they would wear around their waist, and the leaders wore a sash. When a Dog Soldier was attacked, he would stake his rope or sash into the ground, and that's the extent to which he was allowed to move. The only way to be released from duty was by death, or if he was relieved by another Dog Soldier. Anyway, as time passed, their function changed to that of peacekeepers within the tribe."

"Wait, wait, back-up a little here; what about some of the battles I've read-about?" asked Joe. "Now I remember some things about the Dog Soldiers."

"Well, the most well-known was the battle of Greasy Grass River. You know, the Little Big Horn. Dog Soldiers were the first to fight Custer's Seventh Cavalry and continued to fight until all of the Union soldiers were dead."

"I bet they got a lot of scalps that day," said Joe with a smirk.

51

"Only the leaders were allowed to wear human scalps, and they did, along the seam of their buckskin pants," the medicine man said.

"That's heavy stuff."

"The Dog Soldiers didn't bother white settlers or train workers until the Sand Creek massacre in the winter of eighteen-sixty-four, when the Union Army attacked an unarmed group of about one hundred-fifty Cheyenne and Arapaho, mostly women and children, and some elderly men. After that, there were raids all over the northern and southern plains. In the summer of eighteen-sixty-nine, the Union Army's Fifth Cavalry with about one hundred-fifty soldiers and fifty Pawnee scouts attacked twenty Dog Soldiers near Sterling, Colorado, at Summit Springs."

"Not very good odds," Joe said.

"The Dog Soldiers held all of them off until they ran out of arrows, which is when the Pawnee moved in and killed them all. The best known of the Dog Soldiers was Tall Bull, who was killed at this battle. After that, the Union Army conducted the Indian Wars until June of eighteen-seventy-six when all of Custer's men were killed at Little Big Horn."

"That's one hell-of-a-history for the Dog Soldiers," said Joe.

"Fierce fighters to the last man. And I think we need them for what is happening here in Navajo," the medicine man added.

"How will you get them to help?" asked Joe.

"I'll go see them and ask."

Two days later, in Lame Deer, Montana, a man opened a set of heavy wooden doors and directed Eldon through them. He walked into the meeting place of the Council of Forty-four.

A huge table was centered inside the room. Paintings of battle scenes adorned the walls.

The man seated at the head of the table motioned Eldon to an empty seat at the opposite end. He sat down and faced the leader. The forty-four men around the table were silent, and all watched him intently.

Eldon paused for a moment and then thanked the Council for seeing him. The leader waived his hand and prompted him to begin.

He began by telling the Council the same things that he had been telling Joe. "The Navajo Nation is facing a plague of drugs and gang activity People are overdosing and dying. Drugs are plaguing the community. Now it appeared that we are facing a new danger."

An Elder asks, 'What kind of danger?"

He replies, "Arab terrorists are now more than likely hiding in the Nation. The federal authorities seem powerless to do anything. We need the Dog Soldiers to help."

He paused and waited for any questions.

"What do you know about the terrorists??

"Only that they are being sheltered in safe houses in "Navajo."

"What makes you think the drug gangs are involved in this?"

"Daniel Thunder Hawk was one of them."

This caused a stir among the Elders. After a few moments the head of the Council weighed in.

"How do we know the Dog Soldiers won't have trouble with the federal authorities? That seems likely. While we want to help our brothers, we also need to consider the safety of our people. Is now the time for the Dog Soldiers to help?"

Eldon nodded his understanding. The Council was silent, and the leader signaled him again. He got up from his seat when he realized the meeting was over.

He nodded, turned and walked through the doors, and took a seat outside. After what seemed like hours, an emissary came out and told Eldon he would be notified of their decision soon. The emissary smiled and nodded, then turned and walked back inside the Council meeting room, closing the doors behind him.

Eldon had expected a little more information, but understood that he had made an extraordinary request. He headed back to the Navajo Nation.

Joe left his office to go into the field at ten. He had done more research on Begay this morning and made some calls to try and learn more about the situation in Navajo. Eldon called him to tell him the meeting had gone well, and perhaps the Dog Soldiers would be here soon, but there was no guarantee.

Joe decided to pay another visit to Thunder Hawk. He was worried about him, given his recent visit, and the follow up by Begay.

Joe stopped by a local "hole-in-the-wall" shop and ordered a potato and egg burrito and a cup of coffee to go.

A short twenty-five minutes later, he neared Thunder Hawk's house. Thunder Hawk's car was not there.

Damn. This isn't good.

Where would he be?

Thunder Hawk was out on pretrial conditions of release and under "house arrest" because of the cocaine bust. He was not allowed to leave his home except during certain approved hours.

Where was he?

Joe drove around all sides of the house. No car. He radioed dispatch to talk to one of his officers.

No one had any information, and the probation office had not been alerted to anything out of the ordinary. There were no other known addresses for Thunder Hawk. One of the officers told Joe that one of his friends, named James lived close by.

There were no obvious signs of foul play at Thunder Hawk's place. Joe looked for signs of a struggle or problems, but there were none. After getting the address, Joe drove towards James' house.

He rolled past the house and came to an abrupt stop outside of a run-down trailer a half-mile ahead.

Joe climbed two steps and knocked loudly. "James, this is Investigator Joe Eagle! I need to speak with you about Daniel Thunder Hawk! Are you in there?"

No answer. Joe knocked again.

"James, I need to speak with you, are you in there!"

"One second," a shaky voice called out from behind the door.

Moments later, the door opened slightly inward, and James poked his head around the opening. Pungent marijuana smoke poured out of the doorway as James tried without success to disperse it with his hand.

"You aren't going to bust me, are you?"

"James, I need to come in. I'm not here for a marijuana raid. I need information about Daniel Thunder Hawk."

"Come on in."

James opened the door fully, and walked into the living room area. Joe followed him.

The inside of the trailer didn't look much better than the outside. Pizza boxes and beer cans littered the floor. Dirty clothes were flung about all over. A broken clock hung over a couch that looked like it had been picked up off the street somewhere. The smell of marijuana was overpowering.

"Sorry about the mess. Anyway, what do you want to know?"

James plopped down on the couch. It sank as if it had no springs. Joe looked around the room. There was no one else inside.

"James, my name is Joe Eagle, and I am conducting an investigation. I'm trying to find Daniel Thunder Hawk. I think he might be in danger. I just talked to him not long ago. Do you have any idea where he is?"

James started rocking nervously back and forth in his seat. He reached over to a table and grabbed a beer. He took two liberal slugs.

"James, what's going on? Where is Daniel?" Joe spoke with a stern tone.

James appeared to be scared.

"These guys … they came up to us in Sheep Springs … they…" he fumbled over his words.

"Take it easy, James. Whoa. Slow down. Who came up?"

"We were kicking it down at the store. I don't know who they were really. Mexican guys. You knew he was into the drugs, so I'm not telling you anything I shouldn't. It was the guys he ran the drugs for. Gang-bangers. They told Daniel he needed to meet with some guy named Jaime in Farmington, by the Sportsman's

Lounge. I tried to go with him, but he wouldn't let me. I'm really worried. These guys don't mess around, you know?"

James took a huge drink of his beer.

"James, what time was this?"

"Well, this was earlier today. But Daniel left about thirty minutes ago."

James spat out a few more details about what he had seen. Joe quit listening and dodged pizza boxes on his way outside. He opened the door and ran to the car.

Thunder Hawk was in grave danger. Joe knew it. He started the car and floored the accelerator. He made a call to the dispatcher and his supervisor, requesting immediate police support to the area near the Sportsman's Lounge in Farmington. He was racing against time.

Meanwhile, nine men were hidden from view in thick foliage near the San Juan River. Camouflage paint obscured their faces. None of them made a sound. Each of them looked directly in front.

Isha, the leader, was almost six feet tall, with rough looking features, high cheek-bones, and a jutting chin. His dark eyes showed courage, strength, and determination. This was a man who commanded attention.

Thunder Hawk stood in a clearing near the river about thirty yards away. The full moon provided the only light, but any onlooker could see that six armed gang members were surrounding Thunder Hawk. One held a baseball bat. Another wielded double pistols. Jaime stood right in front of Thunder Hawk.

Isha could hear Jaime questioning him about what he had been saying. Jaime waved his .32 caliber pistol in the air and across Thunder Hawk as he spoke. The man next to Isha shifted slightly but noiselessly.

As Thunder Hawk tried to speak up, one of the gang members launched a vicious elbow from behind into the back of his head, opening a gash and knocking him to the ground.

Thunder Hawk grabbed his head and tried to pull himself up. Jaime pointed his .32 at Thunder Hawk's head. Thunder Hawk wouldn't be getting up.

"You messed up real bad, Daniel. You messed up dude."

As he cocked his .32, whatever else Jaime had planned to say would be forever lost to the ages.

At that moment, Jaime's men watched in shock as an arrow like a thunderbolt whizzed through the air and penetrated Jaime's skull, through his right eye, and into his brain. Jaime dropped his gun as if in slow motion and fell to the ground right next to Thunder Hawk. The arrow hit first on its notch and the impact broke it off, leaving the remainder in Jaime's skull. His body twitched a couple of times and then was utterly still.

In the time it takes the brain to process an event, which is completely out of place but carries obvious and sudden danger, adrenaline begins to pump rapidly. As the gang members watched as their leader fell, they entered into a fight or flight mode. They reached for their weapons and tried to look around, but everything slowed down, like they were watching a movie at half-speed. The gang members looked and squinted. Oddly, they thought they were seeing moving shadows.

Were they shadows? Or people? Apparitions that moved violently in and about the group. They couldn't lock on.

What was that?

One gang member raised his gun at what looked like a bear? What the hell? A millisecond later his neck was ripped apart by a slashing knife, and blood spurted all over the ground and onto the gang banger next to him.

More shadows, one resembled a wolf, one a hawk, twisting, surrounding, and moving. Where were they? What were they? Another gang member's head was ripped backwards by a ghost?

Was that an arm slashing his throat?

The gang member watched the knife slash and raised his
bat to swing but couldn't move in time.

His brain wasn't registering that a shiv had just been plunged into the back of his neck, at the base of his brain stem.

"The ghost seemed to move with rhythm," he thought, as he dropped the bat and joined the other gang member in a death fall.

In a matter of seconds, they were all laying on the ground. One struggled to raise his head, and the last thing that he saw was a sash, hanging from the waist of a ghost wolf.

When Joe reached the parking lot of the Sportsman's Lounge he saw, near the river a short distance down, two cars parked at the top of the road. One of them was Thunder Hawk's. Both cars were empty. He glanced around the cars and down the hill.

Due to the proximity, Joe knew that they had taken Thunder Hawk to the San Juan River, which was the most notable natural landmark in that area. Joe floored it and a short distance later topped a hill and screeched to a stop. He threw open the door of his car and began running down a trail towards the river. Joe drew his pistol. He looked through the foliage and trees for any signs of people.

"Holy shit. Oh man."

Joe whispered out loud to himself as soon as he saw it.

His PTSD flared again, and he tried to breathe through it.

The scene was macabre. Bodies lay at odd angles in a circle on the ground. One man's neck was severed almost clean through to the other side. Another man's arm was broken and hung at a horrific angle near his dead body. Blood stained the earth in a pool around the men, and trickles streamed out of their bodies and formed one large pool of dark red.

Joe started to vomit but was able to overcome the urge. He slowed to a walk, fearful that Thunder Hawk must be amongst the fallen.

When he got to the bodies, Joe turned each body over to see the face. The carnage was sickening. Whoever had caused it had used surgical, but deadly precision. Someone definitely knew how to kill. Thunder Hawk was not amongst the fallen. Joe looked around and saw no more bodies.

Thunder Hawk was gone.

Underneath the last body, however, Joe thought he saw a broken arrow. He moved closer and sure enough, it was an arrow. He turned the man over to see his face. There, in his crushed right eye, was the business end of the arrow. He glanced a little further past the dead man, and then he saw it. A ceremonial sash, nailed to the ground by a single arrow. It hit him. He glanced closely at the symbol, a symbol of courage, and of resilience and death. And he knew what it meant. Again the words of the medicine man hit him.

The sash.

The Dog Soldiers are here.

CHAPTER 7

The Dog Soldiers left the San Juan area holding a limp Daniel Thunder Hawk. The trauma of the event had caused him to pass out. He didn't wake until they got to Montana.

In Montana, for the next several days, women nursed Thunder Hawk back to health. He ate heartily and drank several cups of strong tea every day and his strength grew.

A week later, Thunder Hawk arose and walked outside to get some fresh air. As he stretched his limbs and breathed in the crisp Montana air, he looked around.

In front of a house approximately one hundred yards away, he saw the man who had picked him up off of the ground, Isha, and another young Dog Soldier, Asija. They watched him for a few seconds, and then walked over.

Isha said, "Daniel, we're glad to see that you're healing. It's almost time for your training to begin."

"My training?"

"Yes, Daniel. You will become a Dog Soldier, just like your father. He was a warrior. You should know that I didn't want to train you. I don't think that you have what it takes to be a Dog Soldier. Your head is not there right now, but the Council has asked me to do so, for the sake of your father, so it falls upon you to carry on his legacy if you can complete the training."

"My dad was a Dog Soldier?"

Daniel's face scrunched up. He was clearly puzzled now. His dad had spoken of the Dog Soldiers when he was young. He had talked about what great warriors they were, but he had never mentioned that he was a Dog Soldier. To Daniel, he was only a drunk.

"Your father was one of our great men, Daniel. It remains to be seen whether you can live up to his great spirit and his loyalty to his people."

Isha spoke sternly. "If you cannot survive the training, I have no further obligation to you, and frankly, I don't care either way."

Daniel could tell that Isha meant what he said. Asija looked on solemnly, silent as the conversation died. He had the same indifferent look that Isha had.

He motioned for Daniel to follow. He looked back at the house where the women had helped him, and then he strode forward, following Isha.

The training was the most intense thing that Daniel had ever experienced.

It began the first morning at 4:30, when Isha rousted Thunder Hawk out of bed. As he groggily opened his eyes, Isha yelled at him. "Get up. Get up!"

His adrenaline flowed, and he leaped out of bed, thinking there was some emergency. Isha threw clothes at him and said, "You have one minute to get ready."

A minute later on the nose, Isha came back inside and screamed at him. "Get moving!"

He struggled to pull on his shirt. He made it outside not too far behind Isha.

It was still dark. The moon provided just enough illumination so that Thunder Hawk could see the path in front of him.

Just ahead in a clearing, approximately thirteen Dog Soldiers were warming up and stretching. Isha motioned him over and directed Thunder Hawk to follow their lead. After a few minutes passed, the leader of the group, Asija, began running at a brisk pace down a dirt path towards the East. Thunder Hawk tried to jog at first, but quickly fell back fifty yards behind the group.

Isha came up behind him. "Hurry up Thunder Hawk! What's wrong with you! Catch up!"

He ran faster and felt his lungs begin to burn. He was definitely not used to this. His early mornings were usually spent sleeping, after a night of boozing and drugs and women. Now what the hell was this?

The group ran faster, almost at a sprint. Isha was still yelling for him to keep up as he started slipping further behind. They ran three miles, at a 5:30-per-mile pace. At the end of the run Thunder hawk was exhausted.

His stomach heaved twice, and he buckled over and stopped, hands on his hips. He bent down and threw up several times, as Isha stood over him yelling.

"You think you can be one of us? You can't even run! This is day one Daniel. Day one!"

He couldn't think as his body involuntarily reacted to the physical and mental stress. Suddenly his knees buckled, and he fell forward and began crying. It started softly at first, and then grew louder and more intense.

"I want to change. I want to change. I can be better than this."

"Shut up Daniel! Go back to your drugs! Go back to your easy life. WE DON'T NEED YOU."

Isha kicked him as he rolled over onto his side, and kicked him again.

The other Dog Soldiers had run back and were watching. Asija grabbed Isha around the arms and pulled him backwards. Another Dog Soldier stepped forward to help Asija hold Isha. They looked on as Daniel sobbed, holding his head in his hands, mumbling about changing.

Something was beginning to stir in Thunder Hawk following that first day. The next several days would be much the same. Early mornings and very late nights. He studied constantly when he was not in direct training. Isha handed him a volume of materials on historical Dog Soldier battles, training, culture and secret coded language.

Isha told him, "You will learn all of this by the end of your training; or you will fail."

He stayed up most nights until 3:30 a.m., memorizing all the material he was given.

After running for a minimum of five to seven miles every day, the Dog Soldiers introduced Thunder Hawk to ancient exercises and stretching. They did yoga, judo, jujitsu, wrestling, and disarming an opponent.

One particularly adept Dog Soldier worked with him in stick and knife fighting. Isha and the other Dog Soldiers taught Thunder Hawk hand-to-hand combat techniques. They beat him bloody several times in boxing matches and jujitsu contests. Then they taught him firearms training, tracking, and military tactics.

Slowly, Thunder Hawk got tougher. Mentally the runs were not a problem anymore; his lungs were becoming acclimated. He got leaner and started to fight back.

One day, Isha convened a battle among the Dog Soldiers with small stick batons. Thunder Hawk was matched against Asija. When the match started Asija landed a quick blow across his nose and opened up a large cut. His nose bled badly. Within thirty seconds, Asija began hitting him at will, and Thunder Hawk felt the bruises welling up in his arms and legs.

Two minutes into the fight, he looked over at Isha, who was shaking his head and smirking, obviously content that Asija was beating him.

He flashed back to his dad, who would do that sometimes. It had made him think that he couldn't measure up. This memory brought out repressed rage.

Out of nowhere, he began swinging the stick in a rage. He hit Asija on the side of his leg, caught him across the chin and rained blows on him.

He was able to resist and move at first, but then he fell. Thunder Hawk pounced and hit him hard in the head. He raised up to hit him again and felt a huge blow on the back of the head. His world went dark.

After what seemed like hours, Thunder Hawk awoke in a bed. His head felt like it weighed a thousand pounds. He was groggy and then felt something, reached up and realized there was a bandage on his head. He opened his eyes and saw Isha and Asija on both sides of the bed.

"Where am I?"

Isha responded, "You are alright, Daniel. You are safe here. Your training is almost done. You showed some promise for the first time. Maybe you do have some of the same spirit as your father. You need to learn to contain your emotions, and then you will achieve your potential."

"What will happen to me now?"

"You will go through the rest of our ceremony. Then we will close out your training."

The next three days, they told him ancient secrets of the Dog Soldiers and their ways. Towards the end, they led him into a sweat lodge. He sat inside while superheated rocks turned the kiva into a scorching sauna. He meditated and let his mind wander.

Thunder Hawk again felt his dad's presence. Tears began to fall, like when his dad had died, it was a powerful emotion. It wasn't pain or anger or loss. This emotion was one of healing and forgiveness. In the moment when he felt his dad the closest, he thought he saw his dad reach out and touch him on the cheek. He experienced a wave of elation, calmness, love and pride. Pride in his dad, and in his newfound strength.

The next morning, Isha led him into the middle of a circle for the final part of the ceremony. This would be a sun ceremony and would signify the end of his training.

A large post was centered in the ground. Rocks surrounded the post. A fire burned a short distance away. Dog Soldiers stood around the post watching.

Isha stripped Thunder Hawk of his clothes. He wore only a cloth around his waist.

Isha reached up and grabbed ropes attached to the pole. On the end of the ropes were large curved eagle's talons. Isha shoved the talons through the skin and muscle in Thunder Hawk's upper chest. He grimaced but did not cry out.

Isha then leaned him backwards, and the talons started pulling against his chest muscles.

The Dog Soldiers chanted ancient songs about the deeds of their warriors. They asked their ancestors to join in, to bring another man into their warrior society. As the chants grew louder, the talons pulled harder. He grimaced once, but through the pain, he was starting to feel something else. He felt light in his spirit. Although his eyes were closed, he could now see his dad.

He spoke: "*I am sorry my son. I failed you. But now you must not fail your people.*"

Thunder Hawk tried to speak.

Without warning, the talons tore the flesh and tissue and blood spurted out. He fell backwards from the ropes, screaming out in pain right before he hit the ground.

The clouds broke and the sun shone through. Isha picked him up from the ground and the Dog Soldiers made a circle and embraced him as one of theirs, as he cried again.

The next day, Isha led him up to the side of a mountain. Isha had a canvas with him, and he held a brush in his hand. He motioned for Thunder Hawk to take a seat on a rock. Isha also sat down. He positioned his canvas away from the glare of the sun and then Isha began to paint. Hours passed as Thunder Hawk sat and watched as a scene slowly emerged.

A forest was the backdrop. Several large trees were burning. Smoke was inside the forest. Inside a particular grove of trees, Isha painted a curved sword, a particularly menacing looking blade. On the side of it, he painted a sash. The sash was larger and more prominent and in front of the whole scene.

Isha's brush outlined a falling cherry blossom, the symbol of the Samurai.

When he finished, Isha got up pointed to the painting, and told him "Study it."

Without saying another word, Isha turned and walked away.

CHAPTER 8

The FBI office in Albuquerque is located off Interstate 25 in a heavily guarded, modern-looking structure.
On this day, it was bustling with activity: Washington
D.C. and the Attorney General were keenly interested in
developments with "Operation Pipeline."

Special Agent Maria Spencer has been briefing her
supervisor on the status of her investigation and the results of her interviews.

She had joined the FBI three years earlier and rose
very quickly in the ranks because of her work ethic, intelligence, legal background and her uncanny ability to see
through the B.S. to what was really happening in any giv-
en situation.

The "old guard" FBI liked and respected her, even
though she was a woman in what was largely an all old
man's clique.

Her father served in the military with the 82nd Airborne Division, and perhaps did some work for the Central Intelligence Agency, but she wasn't sure. He did
stints in Italy and Spain, something involving Basque
separatists.

Her mother, Luciana, was an Italian beauty, a real
head-turner, as headstrong as they come. She inherited
her mother's good looks, long black hair and brown eyes.
Luciana pushed her hard growing up, and she sailed
through Georgetown's foreign-service program and Yale
law school. She spoke Italian, Spanish, and had a work-

ing knowledge of Russian after minoring in Russian studies at Georgetown.

After a short time working on constitutional law issues at a big firm in D.C., Maria realized that it wasn't for her.

She had her father's interest in the world, and she interviewed for the FBI. Three years later, she was an Agent and assigned to the Narcotics and Anti-Terror Multi-Agency Task Force within the Albuquerque office. She was a fireball, and everyone knew it.

Spencer headed down the hall to the FBI war room with her second cup of coffee. On the walls she'd hung various charts, phone toll analyses, and a "link chart." The link chart contained names and faces and details of her case, dubbed "Operation Pipeline."

She placed a sticky note with the name "Thunder Hawk" on the "drug distribution" headings. The "Drug source" column held a large photo and description of Luis Beltran and his suspected cartel contacts, and his alias was *"El Tiburón."*

The FBI considered him a high value target after he earned the dubious distinction of being named to the FBI's top ten most wanted list.

They suspected him of distributing drugs, smuggling loads of people, running guns to Mexico, and committing various murders, dating back several years. The feds also believed that he was assisting in a large international money-laundering scheme, although the details of that were still pretty sketchy.

Spencer added to the chart the facts surrounding Thunder Hawk's distribution of drugs within Navajo Indian Country.

Next to the link chart, Spencer placed a large map of the Navajo Nation that marked where drug seizures had been made over the past three years.

Although various low level transporters had been prosecuted, none of them had ever talked or cooperated until Thunder Hawk, although something was bothering her.

Her informants had been saying for months that drug gangs were smuggling illegal immigrants into Indian country. The informants were also saying that the immigrants were Arab, and they had possible links to terrorist activities.

Based on this information, Spencer tried to obtain wiretaps on the phones of cartel members and suspected terrorists. The FBI being the bureaucracy that it was, however, her supervisors had flatly denied the request, and told Spencer to continue to focus on the "traditional methods" of investigation. It was about the money.

The way that the FBI worked, stats, arrests, especially drug arrests, and even low-level, made for key numbers that were submitted to headquarters every quarter. These numbers were crunched against numbers from other FBI offices across the country. Congress approved funds based on those numbers, regardless of the significance of the particular case.

Spencer was endlessly frustrated by the reliance on numbers. She had long believed that given carte blanche authority to run an operation like she knew she could – within the confines of the Patriot Act and the Constitution-- she would literally clean things up. It was her mother's relentless drive coming out.

Sadly, her mom had died two years before of lymphoma. Cancer. It was a curse word to her now. She had not recovered from her mother's death yet. As part of her healing, she threw herself into running. She raised money from friends, from time to time, and ran six marathons in two years for the Leukemia and Lymphoma Society (LLS). She planned to run several more; it was her way to fight against the disease that had taken her mom.

Her work was her other source of solace. She wasn't married and didn't have a boyfriend. Actually, she had only dated three guys in her life, if the one-week fling in Florida counted. None of the relationships had worked out. Her work was her passion.

With the information she had obtained, Spencer believed strongly that she had one of the biggest cases of her career.

Near the war room, in another secure area, several desks were newly set up around a group of folding tables, two-abreast, to make one huge surface.

Pre-existing cubicles remained the domain of agents permanently assigned to the office; the desks were for several agents who had been temporarily assigned to Albuquerque for Operation Pipeline. Main Justice had just assigned two additional prosecutors to the case.

The night before, Special Agent in Charge, (SAC) Harold Bowman notified Agent Spencer that he would like to meet with her first-thing in the morning. She arrived at the office at 7:00 a.m.

Bowman had worked for the Bureau his entire adult life. It had not always been easy, given that he was African-American. He experienced racism throughout his career, but chose to fight through it.

Having worked in several locations around the country, and a couple in U.S. held territories, he never questioned an assignment. When he asked to be assigned to

Albuquerque, it was done, but not as just an agent. This time, he was rewarded for his fight. The FBI promoted him to Special Agent in Charge (SAC). It was a fitting end to a career of a dedicated employee.

He greeted her cheerfully. "Good morning, Maria!"

"Good morning. You wanted to see me?"

"I want to show you something in here," he said as they walked.

"Ok, wow, what's all this?" Spencer scanned the room and all of the equipment that had been set up.

"Well, all of this is now your baby. Seems you got the attention of the boys in D.C. It's setup for the extra agents Main Justice said they would send to assist on ... your case," he said.

"How many agents will be added?"

"Ten."

"Good grief," she said.

"Don't worry, Maria. I'll see to it that all involved have no doubt who's running this case, and if you need my help, I
am here to assist you too."

"Thank you, sir."

"Shut the door behind you, Maria."

"Yes, sir," she replies as she closed the door, and then sat at the console next to Bowman.

He began the briefing. "Agents down in Mexico have been onto a money launderer, he's Arab, Lebanese I think, living in Tijuana. He'll be picked up and taken to Juarez tomorrow, and I'd like you to be there to assist in interviews."

"Ah, that's why I'm going down there?"

"Yep. Look, I don't know how much you've worked with agents who spend most of their time out on the frontier, but watch your back; they don't play by the same rules as most of us."

"I will not disgrace the bureau."

"I know you won't. Check in with the SAC in El Paso and he'll let you know the specifics, and where you'll be staying. Keep in touch. Oh and it looks like you won't have much problem getting your wiretaps from here on out. Good work."

With that, Spencer got up, thanked Bowman, and left. She prepared to be gone for a week, but imagined it wouldn't be more than a couple of days. After grabbing her go-bag and some additional clothes, she was headed for the Albuquerque International Airport, destination El Paso.

Spencer arrived at the El Paso FBI office shortly after noon to meet with Special Agent in Charge, Samuel "Sam" Garza.

She introduced herself to the receptionist and asked to see Mr. Garza. She held up her ID to the bullet-proof glass.

"Yes ma'am, Mr. Garza told us to be looking for you. I'll let him know you're here."

Spencer thanked the woman and sat in the lobby briefly before a door opened.

"Agent Spencer, please come in, I'm Sam Garza."

Agent Garza was taken slightly aback: she was far better looking than anyone had let him know.

"Thank you, sir."

"With all that's happening along the border, I hardly get the chance to go to Albuquerque. I don't believe we've met."

"No sir, I don't believe so."

"Please, in my shop, I prefer Sam."

"Call me Maria."

"Have a seat. You need any coffee, tea?"

"No thanks, I'm fine."

"As Hal already explained to you, a couple of Arabs in Mexico have been identified as members of Hezbollah."

He slowly pushed a file-folder toward her.

"I think you'll find what you need in this file we compiled over the last month, so this information is fairly recent."

"Tomorrow at about 8:00 a.m., they will pick Abdullah Bashir up in Tijuana and bring him to Juarez. Arrangements have been made to escort you to where he will be taken, so you should be here around ten. In the meantime, Clara, our receptionist, has directions to your hotel. Everything has already been set up from Hal's office budget, so don't worry about paying for anything."

"Thank you, sir. See you in the morning."

Spencer shook hands and walked out of Garza's office and to Clara's desk.

"What a nice boss you have Clara, and a sense of humor to boot!"

"You should see him when he's not stressed out," Clara said as she handed an envelope to Spencer with her hotel card and directions.

After getting a quick bite to eat in the hotel restaurant, Agent Spencer tossed her bags on the second bed in

the room and changed into some sweats. She opened a bottle of cran-apple juice and a bag of her favorite indulgence, Bold Chex-
Mix, and started to read the unclassified version of the file.

Lebanese born, Abdullah Bashir was thirty-seven years-old, born in Beirut. As a young man he went to school in Beirut, and then attended college in Amman, Jordan, where he got a degree in accounting. Returning home, he couldn't find work, but along the way, he was recruited to help Hezbollah. His parents cautioned him against it, but his mind was set; he agreed with their ideology and the pay was good, and he would travel.

Spencer turned on her computer and ran various Google searches. She accessed the deep web to search for information. Aside from a few news articles on suspected laundering activities by Bashir, there wasn't much to be gleaned from publicly available sources.

Her phone buzzed. She looked down at the text. It was Ryan, her last boyfriend. She hadn't heard from him in a few months. Weird.

Dinner later?

Maria paused and wondered whether she should even text back. Then she punched out a quick text:

Sorry, I can't I'm in El Paso maybe next time.
His response: OK. Have a good trip.

76

Ryan was fun, and she had thought there was something there, but over time her work had gotten in the way.

Maria reflected for a moment and then went back to reading. No point in dwelling on things. Nothing worked out in that area of her life. No time.

As she turned off the lights, she had butterflies in her stomach. Eager to see what happened next in the investigation, she tossed and turned that night and couldn't wait for the next day to begin.

CHAPTER 9

The streets of Tijuana are always busy, and this morning was no different. *La Libanesa* café, a meeting place for people from the Middle East, was especially busy.

Abdullah Bashir was seated at a table, sipping a cup of *Ahweh*, a very strong Lebanese coffee and reading an Arabic newspaper. On the front page there was a picture of armed members of Hezbollah with AK-47s raised in the air.

The two men who were seated at a table close by had been watching Bashir for several minutes. At the appointed time they stood, hurriedly walked to Bashir's table, and greeted him. Bashir instantly froze. The two men surrounded him and instructed Bashir to keep his hands in front of him on the table.

Outside, an SUV slowly approached and parked across the street. One block down on either side of the shop, on side streets, soldiers were stationed, ready for an immediate response. Military Humvee's displaying M-60 machine guns in turrets rolled into their assigned spots.

"We're agents of the United States government. You are under arrest. We are taking you to Juarez, where you will be interviewed about your activities against the United States of America."

"You don't have jurisdiction here, I'm not going anywhere with you!"

Bashir stood up to leave, but a third man blocked his way.

"I'm Roberto Garcia-Altez of the PGR, Mexican Attorney General's office and I have authorized these men to take you into custody and remove you to Juarez. Do you have any questions?"

"No."

"Then please come with us outside, quietly."

The men each held one of Bashir's arms and escorted him out. They put him in the back seat where one of the agents got in and sat next to him. Mr. Garcia-Altez got into the front seat for the ride to Tijuana International Airport, to make sure all went well, at least until they boarded their private jet.

"Where are you taking me?"

"No talking," the agent seated next to him said briskly.

"But you already said you were taking me to Juarez."

"No talking," he said. This time he had a more aggressive tone and manner.

This is going to be a long trip, Bashir thought to himself.

Now in Juarez, Bashir looked out and could see a cold-looking gray building that resembled a prison. There were no signs in or around the building. The Mexican federal police owned it.

"If you need the bathroom, use it now; he will accompany you," the agent said gesturing toward the driver who had taken them to Juarez.

"I do need the bathroom, but I don't need an escort."

"Suit yourself."

After Bashir emerged, the agent led him into a room without furniture or windows. There were no chairs. The entire room was concrete. "Sit down!" the agent yelled.

"I should have guessed," said Bashir. "This is a torture chamber."

"Sit down, I told you!"

The door opened.

"Hey, someone needs to see you," the agent said. As he walked toward the door, he remarked, "Get this place ready, we're going to have a party!"

As he went out, two others entered the room. One carried two saw horses and a plastic gallon bottle of water. The other had two pieces of two inch by twelve boards with several straps and buckles hanging from them. The men sat the boards on the sawhorses; one of them was taller than the other.

Bashir was now crouched in a corner of the room, wide-eyed at the preparations being made. As three men approached him, he objected and his voice rose as they grabbed him.

He continued to protest as the men dragged him to the make-shift table and placed plastic cuffs on his wrists, hands in front of him.

Bashir struggled mightily, but the men were too strong for him. He was shouting, "No! Please! Do not to do this!"

"Don't fight this, man. It ain't going to do any good. We're going to introduce you to the concept of dying, and then we'll take a break. After you catch your breath, we'll do it all over again. At some point we are going to allow you to answer our questions. If you do, this can all stop."

"For the sake of *Allah*, why don't you just ask me the questions? I don't know what you want!"

One of the men quickly put a black hood over Bashir's head.

"What are you doing, leave me alone; I have not done anything wrong," he was crying and pleading with them.

"Back up slowly until you feel the board." the man said ominously.

Bashir fell straight down, like he had been shot.

"Shit, he passed out!"

"I guess he doesn't like the hood," one of them said, and they laughed.

"Let's get him up onto the boards; we need to have him ready when the boss gets back."

"What the hell are you doing?!"

The men looked up and were surprised to see a woman screaming at them. Spencer now stood an arm's length away, visibly upset at what she was looking at.

One of the men snarled, "You can't be in here. You're gonna have to leave, lady."

"I said, what the hell do you think you're doing?"

One of the guys on the other side of the rack walked toward her slowly. Like a predator, he sized up his prey.

"Don't pick a fight you can't finish," she said as she dropped her tablet to the floor and stepped back into a forty-five degree angle, fighting pose.

The man in front of her prepared to step forward.

"Stand down. Stand down!"

A senior agent who had just entered the room behind Spencer was visibly agitated as he yelled at them all.

"She's FBI, and here from D.C. What's going on here?" the senior agent asked in a manner as self-composed as he could be.

"We were going to interrogate him," the man said.

"By fucking water-boarding him!" Spencer yelled.

"It's what we do," he said with a puzzled look.

"Not today you don't, cut him loose. I'm taking him to El Paso."

"You can't just take him out of the country. You'll create an international incident."

"That's exactly what we are going to do. Fix it so we can!"

Spencer took out her cell phone and dialed.

"I am contacting the Mexican AG's office, and there won't be any torture of this man."

"Here." the senior agent said.

"This is the personal number of the deputy AG for the state of Chihuahua. I'll ask him to fast-track authorization for you through the state department."

"Please have your men bring this man to your conference room after he wakes up."

A short time later, the guards led Abdullah Bashir to the conference room, wearing a pair of coveralls.

He walked in slowly, looking around to see what lay in store for him.

"Mr. Bashir, I'm Maria Spencer, with the FBI."

He stopped walking forward.

"Please, take a seat."

"What does the FBI want with me?" he asked with hesitation as he sat across the table from her. "Are you going to torture me?"

"No," she answered.

She flipped open her embossed Department of Justice notebook, then removed the folder with his information.

"Mr. Bashir, I prefer we talk in a respectful manner with each other. There won't be any torture, but I do expect that you will be cooperative. In turn, you have my pledge that you will not be tortured. Is that fair?"

"Yes."

Spencer began slowly, asking questions to verify the information that the Bureau had on Bashir's background. Bashir hesitated at first but then became more comfortable and answered the questions. Once Spencer was satisfied it was correct, she set the folder aside and prepared to take notes.

"I heard you talking to them about transferring me to another location. Where are you going to take me?"

"Where would you like to go?" she asked.

"I would like to seek asylum in the United States."

"Why?"

"Because now they will kill me if you let me go."

"Who are they?"

"My people or the cartel. Take your pick."

"Why would they want to kill you? Is that what those guys wanted to know? Why don't I call them in here and we can ask them."

"No, no, no please, not on my account," Bashir said as he broke out in a sweat. "What did you say your name is?"

"Special Agent Spencer."

"Agent Spencer, as soon as you get me out of this country and into the United States, I'll tell you everything you want to know."

"That's a sucker's bet, Abdullah."

"You saved me from that room. You have my word."

"This is coming from a man whose own people want to kill him. No sir, I either get my answers now, or I'm headed back into El Paso. It's about a ten minute drive to the border from here, as I recall."

"Yours is a different kind of torture, but torture none the less," he told her.

"At least I'm giving you a choice; more than you got earlier!"

"Yes, yes, you are right, and I do appreciate it. What is it you want to know?"

"Look, I don't have a prayer rug, but its noon and you probably want to pray, or am I wrong."

Bashir relaxed some at this comment. "No, you are correct, but I prayed while I was changing in the bathroom, thank you anyway."

There was a knock at the door and the senior agent popped his head inside.

"Excuse me, but I just got word that your request will go through, but it will take a while. We are pushing for five o'clock today."

"Thank you." Spencer replied

Bashir kept his face down while the man was in the room. He closed the door behind him as he left.

"Allah be with you," he said.

"Thank you."

"Of course," he responded.

They were standing outside the conference room when the senior agent walked back into where they were.

"Authorization came through to take Mr. Bashir to Ft. Bliss. It's also been cleared through ICE for you both to go by helicopter. We have one waiting at the airport."

"Thank you, Agent... Jones, Jack Jones. Really?"

"Naw." He said with a straight face.

"*Touché*, Agent Jones," she said with a smile.

"If you're ready, I'll drive you to the airport."

"Give me just a minute, please." Agent "Jones" left and they walked back into the room.

"Abdullah, before we leave I want your assurance you'll tell me about the smuggling operation you've been running between Brazil and Mexico, and how people are getting across into the U.S., and where they can be located."

"You have my word."

"If you lie to me it's right back here, because there's no record of you ever entering the United States. Do you understand that?" she said.

He paused for a moment, and replied, "You have my word."

The helicopter at Juarez International Airport didn't have any numbers or markings. It was completely black. They flew in complete silence. The ride took all of ten minutes, and they landed at Ft. Bliss Army Base, El Paso, Texas.

CHAPTER 10

Spencer looked out the window of the UH-60 Black-hawk. Rows of houses dotted both sides of the international border between the United States and Mexico. The Juarez side looked exceptionally poor, especially along the *frontera*, where shanty-towns can run for miles. At the border, though, there wasn't a lot of difference between the United States and Mexico.

She wondered what the next several hours would bring. Seated in front of her, under armed guard, was one of the highest value targets that the United States had arrested in recent memory. His information would lead not only to arrests in this case, but also to arrests around the country related to terrorism. Operation Pipeline was reaching a critical juncture.

With the recent information the FBI had gotten from Daniel Thunder Hawk, the Arab connection was getting stronger. She believed that Bashir might be the right person to get the final, and critical piece of information.

The helicopter turned toward Fort Bliss and started its descent.

Fort Bliss sits in the West Texas desert, in El Paso, and is the United States Army's second largest installation. It is the home of the 1st Armored Division and also the home of the El Paso Intelligence Center (EPIC).

EPIC was established in 1974 as a southwest border intelligence center. It contains a repository where vast amounts of intelligence are gathered, analyzed, and stored on drug smuggling, cartel activity and terrorism. The center then makes that intelligence available to law enforcement around the country and the world. It was the perfect site for the interview of an international money launderer who also had ties to terrorism.

The helicopter landed on the empty airstrip. Spencer could see no vehicles or people within eyesight, except an approaching four-vehicle military convoy. As the helicopter shut down, the flight engineer opened the cargo door. Guards covered his head and rushed Bashir quickly out and into the lead vehicle of the convoy. They directed Spencer into the second military vehicle. Two armored vehicles flanked the convoy, and armed soldiers scanned the roadway.

The convoy rolled forward to a large building near Biggs Army Airfield, which was adjacent to the fort. The building was set off and surrounded by concertina wire. As the gates opened, Spencer could see armed security personnel at the entrance. After checking credentials, the guards opened the doors, and everyone proceeded inside.

Inside the building, the doors opened to a spacious warehouse area with tables and chairs in the center. Numerous people operated computers. Marines guarded rooms set off to the sides of the main entrance.

An escort led Spencer to an interview room on the right side of the building. It was spacious, with a large table in the center and several chairs. One-way mirrors on the east wall disguised video and audio systems designed to capture what was being said and happening in the room.

Spencer took a seat at the table, opened her laptop, and sipped coffee out of a Styrofoam cup. Shortly thereafter, two stern Marine MPs led Bashir into the room, and pushed him into the chair across the table from her. Bashir faced the mirrored wall.

The MPs took a few steps backwards and stood behind him, guns at the ready.

"Gentlemen, could you allow us to speak in private? There is no need to watch this man." Agent Spencer spoke with authority.

"Ma'am we are under strict orders to guard this prisoner," the Marine MP stated.

"You can guard him from outside the door."

"We do not have authority to leave this prisoner's side, ma'am."

Spencer was firm. "Call your supervisor, and tell him that the FBI Agent needs to speak to this prisoner without guards present."

After a few calls, the Marine MPs left the room and stood outside the door.

She was alone in the room with Bashir now. She paused to consider the situation and to control her nervousness. She was about to interview the most highly valued target that the United States currently had in custody and she could not afford to mess this up.

The interview started slowly at first. Spencer gathered background information and tried to ease the mood. About a half hour into the interview, she turned to the substance.

"Ok, Mr. Bashir, let's start with the broad outlines, and then I will ask you some specific questions. Tell me how you started laundering money?"

He sat silent and stared ahead at Agent Spencer.

"Mr. Bashir, you have been cooperative to this point, and I expect your further cooperation."

Bashir remained silent and just nodded his head. Spencer waited for a response, but he continued to stare straight ahead.

Spencer slammed her laptop on the table, and the noise made Bashir jump.

"Look, Mr. Bashir I don't really care what happens to you at this point. You are going to talk, or I am done, and you are going back to Juarez. It's your choice. I don't give a damn if you don't like me, if you think you can avoid me. I'm not going away until I get my answers."

Bashir shifted in his seat and stared up at the FBI Agent in front of him. He wondered if she was serious or not.

"If I talk, they will kill me. If I don't talk, your government will torture me. What would you do in my position? I have a family."

"Well, I'm not in your position, Mr. Bashir, but if I were in deep shit like you find yourself right now, I would realize that I'm about the only person in the world you can trust right now."

"What assurances can you give me that my family will be spared if I tell you about all of this?"

Bashir shifted back and forth in his seat.

Spencer hesitated for a moment. "I am authorized to tell you that right now you are facing a certain life sentence, if I walk out of this room, you are charged with international money laundering, as a member of a drug conspiracy, and with ties to terrorists. I am your only hope to ever, and I mean EVER, see the light of day again. You have a family? Do you want to see them again? If you do, then I am your only hope! Do you understand what I am telling you? Your only chance is right here and right now. If I leave and tell them we are done, you are done forever. See what I am saying here? On the other hand, if you are truthful and tell me everything that you know, and what you have done, we can discuss placing you and your family in the Witness Security program only if you are going to talk. I am not going to let you throw your life away today."

Bashir was weakening. "Will I be given asylum, and my family, um, will they get asylum also?"

"We can discuss that, Mr. Bashir, but the first step is for you to be fully truthful. You can't leave anything out, you can't hedge, you can't falsify anything, or I will get up and walk out of here and that will be it. Are we clear?"

Bashir had completely broken and was looking down at the table. When he looked up, Spencer saw the expression of a different man.

"Ok. Ask your questions."

Over the next three hours, Bashir spilled details of his involvement in the complicated money-laundering scheme.

The scheme started with vast amounts of drug money. Smugglers in the organization preferred marijuana and cocaine. They brought the drugs in mainly through the Arizona and New Mexico borders.

There were two methods of smuggling: Mexican smugglers flew ultralight airplanes across the international border, "lights out," below radar and dropped two hundred pound loads of marijuana into remote desert areas for later pick up.

Couriers, usually "backpackers," carried the drugs from there. The backpackers were illegal immigrants who volunteered to pack the drugs in for three hundred dollars per "load." They smuggled the drugs in on their backs and dropped them at preset locations in the desert.

A driver would then pick up all of the backpacks, or bundles dropped from the planes, and take the drugs to a safe house for further distribution into the interior of the country.

The cartel made cash payments to trusted drivers who provided those payments to mid-level cartel members. The cartel then laundered monies through car dealerships across the southwestern United States.

As Spencer questioned him, Bashir gave her answers. It wasn't all the truth, but he felt it was enough to convince the agent to keep her word and get him and his family to the United States. He told Spencer that he set up the laundering scheme, using the car dealerships for one of the cartels.

The scheme, at its height, was able to launder over fifty million dollars a month. He described the various methods, but the main one was through a bank in Canada affiliated with one in Lebanon. In turn, banks used in the Middle East would loan money to people in Europe and the United States to buy more car dealerships.

The dealerships would buy cars and then sell them to people in Europe and Africa. The money went back to the cartel in Mexico.

"Fifty million a month." she said.

"Yes, sometimes more, but rarely less."

Over the past decade, Bashir estimated that the cartel had laundered billions in drug money.

She learned that the drug operation was run by the Mexican cartel, which employed *La Raza*.

The cartel had also smuggled hundreds of guns purchased with drug money back into Mexico, many with the knowledge of the United States, as part of its universally decried, "Operation Fast and Furious."

Spencer had read extensively about "Operation Fast and Furious." The FBI for several years had participated with the Bureau of Alcohol, Tobacco and Firearms (ATF) and the Drug Enforcement Administration (DEA), in that Operation. Agents in Arizona launched it. It was a debacle of a concept. The theory was that the government would allow individuals to smuggle guns illegally into Mexico and then trace and follow the guns so as to locate and identify criminals "higher up" the food chain who were trying to obtain guns. The strategy had failed miserably.

Its creators apparently failed to realize that once the guns made it into Mexico and outside of the United States, the agencies had no way to trace them and so they had lost total control over where the guns went. Estimates were that as many as two thousand guns were allowed to "walk" into Mexico, and were subsequently lost. Worse yet, once the agencies started talking at a higher level, they realized that some of the high-level targets sought by the ATF, were actually informants of the FBI. Congress lambasted the agencies and the Attorney General.

Tragically, the cartel shot and killed border patrol agents, with a gun that the government allowed to "walk" in Operation Fast and Furious. Allegations and rumors abounded that the CIA was involved in the drug and gun smuggling, or allowed it to happen.

It wasn't at all clear to what extent the United States government had its hand in all facets of the cross-border smuggling.

The whole thing made Spencer sick to her stomach. She was determined to get any information that she could from informants to vindicate the agents and others who had been tragically victimized. Most of all, Spencer wanted the truth.

As she turned from her thoughts, Bashir continued to explain that the purpose of the scheme, the whole purpose, was to get money in the hands of terrorists, smugglers who would bring terrorists into the United States who would harm this country.

"The terrorists have been smuggled through tunnels into your country."

"Where are the tunnels?"

"I don't know exactly, but they lead into California, Arizona, and New Mexico. The one in New Mexico is near a train station or train tracks."

Spencer's mind was running at high speed.

Where is that, she wondered. *Train station*?

"The Arabs were taken to the place where the Indians live. They are here for a specific purpose, to destroy your country when it is their time."

"What do you mean, the place where the Indians live?"

Her heart was racing now. She suddenly felt that a stopwatch had been activated, and she was working against it.

"Your reservations. They live on the reservation."

"Which reservation? Which Indian tribe?"

She was pressing him now. New Mexico is home to several Native American tribes, and she knew in addition to the thirteen pueblos where Native Americans live in New Mexico, there were also the Navajo, Mescalero and

Jicarilla Apache reservations. Reservation could mean any of these lands.

"It is in the northern part of New Mexico, in a town called Navajo, that's all I know."

She pressed on. "When is their time, Bashir? When are they going to act? "

"I do not know. I'm sorry. We send money to Central America. They are building a weapon. It will kill many Americans. That's all I know."

Spencer slammed her laptop shut and ran out of the room. When she turned on her phone, she had two voice mail messages. Spencer listened intently as SAC Bowman talked about the leak regarding Daniel Thunder Hawk. The next call was from Joe Eagle, from Navajo Criminal Investigations. Thunder Hawk was missing.

She called her supervisor.

"I need agents in the Navajo Nation immediately. We have terrorists, I repeat terrorists there!"

Her supervisor interrupted: "Whoa what?"

"Yes, that's right, that's what Bashir is saying, and Thunder Hawk has been kidnapped I think. It has to be the cartel. This case has just gotten a lot more important, and I need help right away. We need people on the ground, RIGHT NOW!"

CHAPTER 11

Bashir scanned the room. It was empty. He waited for Agent Spencer or someone else to return.

They will not know the full truth. They will not know all that Agha has planned.

Bashir continued to ponder his situation.

The United States is weak. They are no longer the beacon of hope that it used to be. Now it is full of self-centered, money grubbing politicians. There was no spirit left.

He had read about the revolution, and the will of the Americans when the country was newly formed, in blood. He admired their determination. They took on the giant at the time, Great Britain. A small band of proud warriors. It was a storied and rich history. But no longer.

Americans were weak, too obsessed with their newest iPads and technology and what they could get for themselves. And with all this technology and development, what had become of it? A destroyed land and natural resources and people still broke? An economy in shambles?

This giant, this new giant, the United States of America, would soon become a broken, splintered ailing relic.

Bashir's thoughts were broken by the opening of the door.

"Mr. Bashir, I apologize for having to leave. I had to make a call and did not mean for it to take so long. I would like to get back to what we were talking about."

Bashir eyed Spencer closely. Her mannerisms betrayed something had just happened. He intended to exploit whatever weakness that he could.

When Bashir spoke now his voice had a different, more defiant tone.

"I have spoken with you for over three hours. I have given you information. Yet I have no assurances of anything. I think we have reached the point where you provide those to me or this interview is completed."

Bashir rose upward in his seat in a cocky posture.

Brief anger flashed in her eyes. Just as quickly as it had come, it went away. She knew that terrorists were right now in New Mexico, and that she had to find them. The next few hours were critical. She desperately needed the vile character in front of her, as much as she despised him, to help her do it.

When she spoke, her tone was measured.

"Mr. Bashir, I appreciate the fact that you believe you have some negotiating room here. Let me remind you, you do not. I am in charge of this interview and your freedom. You can choose to have that freedom, or you can choose to go back to Juarez. I suggest you take as much time as you need and think long and hard about what you will choose."

Bashir clenched and unclenched his hands. He looked down to make sure she saw that he was reflecting, and then he looked up again and to the side. Thirty seconds passed as he gently tapped his fingers on the table and then his head.

Then, without warning, Bashir sprang to his feet and grabbed his chair from under him. His eyes glared red with hatred as he swung the metal chair up in an arc and prepared to launch it at Spencer.

She raised her arms and Bashir twisted his body and swung hard at her head. She flinched, ducked down, and instinctively extended her arm to deflect the chair. As she ducked, she leaned left and kicked hard at the laptop, slamming it into Bashir's chest.

He dropped the chair; it clanged loudly on the table and fell to the floor where Spencer had been sitting.

She rolled to her left over her shoulder and grabbed the .9mm from her holster. As she lay on her back everything was moving in slow motion.

She turned towards Bashir and had her eyes locked on his chest, in the center of mass, as her arm raised and she prepared to fire a round.

He was moving forward like a rocket, arms extended and hands clutching for her throat. His eyes reflected death. He saw the gun, dove forward and was in mid-air as he registered in his peripheral vision a large object coming hard at him.

The United States Marine Corps enjoy their reputation as "devil dogs" for a reason. And later when Bashir reflected on the events, he realized that he'd never had a chance.

The very second that he jumped out of his chair and reached to grab it, the two Marines were moving. At the instant Bashir leaped forward, six foot four, two hundred thirty pound Marine Corp Sergeant and ex-linebacker, John Randall, hit him with a vicious shoulder tackle that caused a loud crunching sound.

Bashir felt his ribs crack as he slammed to the floor head-first. Instinctively, Randall raised his fist to punch, but there was no need. Bashir was out cold. He would not come back to consciousness for another three minutes.

Spencer was just milliseconds from pulling the trigger when she too saw the violent collision.

As she rose up from the ground, it looked to her as if Bashir was dead. She took several breaths, as the Marine grabbed her hand and helped her to her feet.

"You ok, ma'am?"

"Yes, yes, I will be ok. Just need a second to catch my breath. And thank you. Is he still alive?"

"He's still breathing ma'am. But he is going to wish he was dead when he wakes up."

After she'd regained her composure, Spencer called for SWAT assistance in Las Cruces, New Mexico.

During those five minutes, a breakthrough was about to be made that would change the world forever –for the worse.

CHAPTER 12

Jaco, Costa Rica, is a beautiful beach and surf town located an hour from San Jose, the capitol of Costa Rica. It boasts some incredible surfing, amazing seafood, and offshore fishing. It has long drawn scores of tourists, where they dot the beaches, watching locals tear up the waves, which were high today.

A fifty-minute boat ride off shore, in a fifty-five foot fishing boat named The *Volk*, five Russian scientists were meeting with members of the most powerful cartel in Mexico.

The waters gently pushed the boat as the sun set over the beautiful Pacific Ocean. A seven-hundred pound blue marlin leaped in the air two hundred yards off the boat, paused effortlessly in mid-flight, then ducked her head and plunged back into the sea, apparently content with this day. The captain, himself a Russian, watched the flight of the marlin, and mused to himself that he would much rather be fishing, but they had paid him handsomely for this trip. Under no circumstances was he to venture into the cabin. His job was to navigate the boat and watch for anyone approaching.

In the cabin were some of the most deadly minds to ever have been assembled in the history of the world. A middleman had carefully handpicked the Russian scientists. Bashir and the men in Iran had chosen the middleman. Bashir was financing this top-secret project, and paying the cartel to provide security, and to set up a lab in Costa Rica.

The cartel had chosen a remote area near Jaco for the lab. To a casual observer, nothing seemed out of sorts. The sign identifying the newest "Eco Lodge" in Costa Rica looked as non-descript as the scores of people near-by wearing beach shorts, but this was no ordinary "Eco Lodge."

In fact, this was the most sophisticated lab that drug and terrorist money could buy. These scientists were some of the most creative and brilliant minds in the world.

In the 1980s and through the early 1990s in post-Cold War U.S.S.R., scientists worked together in a secret lab in Russia to develop various bio-terror weapons. They experimented with botulinum toxin, the plague, smallpox, and various other deadly viruses and germs. Despite an international treaty banning it, the scientists conducted live tests on monkeys on a secret Island in the Aral Sea.

In addition to working with known bio-terror agents, the scientists also worked to combine various types, like the plague and smallpox for instance, to create a virus called a chimera.

In Greek mythology, the chimera was a monster made from parts of different animals. A chimera virus, similarly, was made from two or more microorganisms.

Some of these scientists were now in Jaco. They worked for years on their current project. The cartel paid them handsomely to create another chimera virus.

By experimentation over time, the scientists realized that they could genetically alter smallpox. Several parts of the smallpox genome or DNA could be used to intro-duce foreign genetic material. The scientists learned that the Ebola virus uses RNA for its genetic code, while smallpox uses DNA. Through trial and error, they were able to make a DNA copy of Ebola and splice it into the receptive parts of the smallpox virus.

The result was a super deadly combination virus of Ebola and smallpox. As a combination, the virus creates "blackpox," known as hemorrhagic smallpox, its most deadly form. In a blackpox infection, the skin becomes dark, all over. Blood vessels leak, resulting in severe internal hemorrhaging. Internal organs literally liquefy one by one. Afflicted persons will hemorrhage blood and melted organs everywhere, including through their eyes and orifices. The mortality rate is almost one hundred percent, and the addition of the smallpox makes the virus highly contagious. In short, this chimera virus—dubbed Ebola-pox by the scientists—was as deadly as they come.

What these scientists did not have was money to research further – until Bashir. This research was needed to weaponize the Ebola-pox.

The idea was to create a dust cloud of fine particles that could be introduced into the air, preferably a closed air system, and coat a large group of people, killing as many as possible, quickly and effectively. But the problem for creating a weaponized chimera virus had long been the same – the organisms could not be made into a powder which could be released into the air while sustaining their deadly properties. This powdered form was necessary for any type of release from a weapon, be it an airplane or a dirty bomb.

There was also the problem that sunlight would destroy any weaponized virus released into the air. No one had ever figured out how to complete this last piece of the puzzle. That is, until now.

The sole purpose of the Costa Rican lab, as envisioned by Ahmed, Bashir and their terrorist colleagues, was to hire the best scientists that money could buy to figure out how to weaponize the virus. It was a twist on the United States' "Operation Paper Clip" in WWII.

Following the fall of Germany and the end of WWII, the United States employed a program to either terminate German scientists if they wouldn't come to the United States, or to extradite those that would. The United States quietly extradited many German scientists to the military base at White Sands, New Mexico. Over decades, they worked to help create some of the most sophisticated spy aircraft that the United States ever built.

Following suit, Bashir paid millions to recruit his team of preeminent scientists. The trick had taken quite a long time to figure out.

The scientists finally learned how to manipulate parts of the DNA of the Ebola pox to add mass in order to create a fine, almost un-detectible powder, which could be placed in a bomb, or an aerosol container that could be sprayed into any closed air system, such as an airplane or at a mall, ensuring maximum distribution over a large group of people.

As a result, on this day, the scientists toasted and cheered the most deadly, earth-changing weapon since the first nuclear bomb had exploded at the Trinity Site in New Mexico. The breakthrough occurred at approximately the same time Agent Spencer was giving Bashir his ultimatum.

The scientists placed the call to the cartel contact after their discovery. They arranged to come together later that day and assemble on the boat. The cartel contact sent a coded message to Ahmed and received his orders. All were extremely pleased.

Now, inside the cabin of the boat were two couches. A table in between held several bowls of fresh fish and some beers. Towards the back end of the cabin, a staircase led below to the head. A television adorned the wall opposite the scientists, but no one was watching.

"We're done. We've finalized the weapon, and it can be delivered to you. We now require our last payment of one-hundred-million and we will turn over all of the contents to you."

The Russian scientist smiled as he related their discovery to the cartel members. His colleagues nodded.

"Are the contents completely sealed as we were promised? They must travel a long way, and we need them to make it there."

The cartel member had an icy demeanor. "Where is the product? You are aware we will not pay until we receive the product?"

"I understand," The scientist said. "It is safe in containers one mile from the lab, where you asked us to store it. We can deliver it immediately upon confirmation that the money is transferred."

The cartel member rose from his seat and walked out of the cabin to the hull of the ship.

His satellite phone registered service. The sun had completely dipped, and the night-light shone on the water. He placed a quick call.

"It is ready. Go to the location. Now. Tell me when you are there."

He hung up and strode back down into the cabin.

"In minutes my men will be there. We have always kept our word. When the containers are handed over, I will make one call, which you can watch, and your money will be transferred immediately. It is waiting transfer as we talk."

"That is acceptable."

The scientist shifted a little uneasily in his seat. It was always this way at the end, wondering who would show his hand first.

Minutes later, the cartel member's phone lit up.

"They are there. Direct them to deliver the containers, and the money is yours."

The scientist stepped out unto the hull and made a call. Across the water and near the lab, the man acknowledged the call. He hung up and signaled to his comrades.

Then, they slowly and carefully began to hand airtight metal containers, which contained aerosol containers of the weaponized Ebola-pox to the cartel members. The deadly powder within the aerosol containers was enough to kill hundreds of thousands, even millions of people, because of its deadly contagiousness. The men on the other side of the transaction gingerly accepted the airtight containers.

The scientist walked back into the cabin.

"It is done. The transfer has been made."

The cartel member's phone again lit up as soon as the statement was made.

"Thank you for your service. You have all been instrumental to the cause. It is too bad that you won't see the results."

The cartel member rose. He raised a gun and pointed it at the chief scientist as his associates pointed guns at the others. The scientists' faces went ashen. They tried to move run, but they couldn't react quickly enough. In one frightfully efficient and violent moment, each cartel member trained his laser sights on the forehead of a scientist and fired two bullets.

As the scientists crumpled and died inside the boat, their colleagues who had handed over the Ebola-pox were also taking their last breaths. The last bullet made its way through the back of the head of the shocked Russian captain, an innocent bystander, but a potential witness who had to be eliminated.

Gentle waters rocked the boat. The boat shifted in those vast, dark waves of the ocean. The corpses were cut and thrown over the boat into the ocean, to be consumed by the sharks, as the fruits of their deadly efforts, the virus, began to make its journey northward.

Within a week, the cartel transported the virus through Nicaragua to an Arab stronghold in southern Mexico, and then, with the assistance of a Mexican general, through Mexico and to a safe house in Juarez, which was heavily guarded.

The deadly chimera virus would remain there, less than a mile from the United States border of El Paso, Texas, until the Arabs gave the signal that it was time.

CHAPTER 13

When Bashir came back to focus, Spencer was before him as if in a dream.

"You son of a bitch! You're lucky you aren't dead now, you piece of shit!"

Bashir raised his hands to his head, and she smacked them off.

"I need this information now, or this is the end for you, you worthless bastard. I need to know where your associates are! Now!"

Spencer's cocked firearm was now pressed against Bashir's forehead as he began to plead for his life. When he opened his mouth, he was trembling. "They are with the Navajo Indians. In the Navajo Nation. That's all I know. I swear on the lives of my kids. I swear to you. Please ..."

"What are they going to do Bashir? What?"

"They will fly planes, the ultralights, into your country and drop the deadly weapon onto your country. *In sha'Allah.*"

She was already running out of the room.

"I need the team, every agent you have, all of them now! Navajo! They are there, the terrorists are in Navajo! Go now!" Spencer barked into her phone and across the line orders were already being given.

The FBI SWAT team was already geared up and ready to go. It took one call, and they were alerted that the mission was an immediate go.

They were en route within an half-hour to the Navajo Nation. With them were the state police, local SWAT and quick response units. With any luck, they would be quick enough to stop the terrorists.

In the dead of night, in the safe house in Navajo Village, the Arabs huddled together, waiting quietly for the signal from their handlers that it was time to leave. Their stay had not been unpleasant.

Begay arranged for a local older Navajo woman to cook for them and bring them their meals. She also regularly cleaned their linens. There were makeshift bunk beds placed side by side in the two living areas. The jihadists were able to go outside for brief periods at night to get fresh air, but only in groups of two.

The Arabs had watched the gang members now for months. In recent days it was becoming apparent that they were not the kind of professionals the Arabs were used to working with. They'd overheard talk that some of the gang had been executed at a nearby river.

These were petty thieves, not up to the task. When the gang members had seen the police in Navajo, they had shown panic and indecision, and it made Agha nervous. It was not the calm disposition that professionals show, even in stressful situations.

Looking around the room in the dim light, Agha saw the faces of his fellow Jihad warriors and felt pride in his heart. Some were looking straight ahead, some were looking down, and some wrung their hands together. All were focused. He carefully chose each for this mission because of their skills and their laser-like focus on the task ahead of them.

"Praise Allah", Agha thought, these warriors, and the sleeper cells they would awaken, would unleash death

107

upon the Americans in numbers that would dwarf the mayhem of 9-11.

For over a decade, "sleeper cell" terrorists quietly entered the United States, obtained jobs and worked, patiently waiting to be called into action to attack Americans. Agha had long dreamed of this moment. This attack would again expose America's vulnerability.

He softly cursed the incompetence of the Americans, and despised the weak men who now were his only way out of this safe house and the Navajo reservation.

Agha told his warriors once the pathetic gang members transported them out of the safe house and to another location, they would find a way to leave them, and if it took killing them, well, that is what would be done. This mission would be accomplished at all cost.

The door opened above and more light shone into the room. Agha raised his hand to his eyes. The gang member waved. It was time to leave.

As the Jihadist's left the basement and headed outside to the SUVs, Agha paused and took a long look around him into the night.

The stars shone over him and the village and the houses. This land, this land of opportunity, as they say, reminded him of home, or at least the terrain was similar. He took a deep breath and smiled as he realized he was actually here, in the land of his enemy.

The lion is inside the den with the lambs, Agha mused, *and they are powerless to stop the slaughter.*

The quietness and stillness of the night sky and air was a stark contradiction to the violence that must soon follow.

It was the calm before the storm.

108

Agha slid into the SUV and was about to enter the false floor when he spotted two young Native Americans smoking cigarettes and watching what was happening from about thirty-five feet away.

He calmly stood back up, exited the SUV, and pulled a cigarette from his pocket. The other Arabs rose up to see what was happening. Their faces registered surprise and shock as Agha began walking towards the young men.

As Agha extended his hand and held out his cigarette, presumably wanting a light, the older of the youths got up and pulled a Bic out of his pocket. As he moved his thumb to fire the flame, Agha also moved swiftly with his curved blade. It cut at a sickening angle from right to left and almost severed the head of the young kid who was trying to light the cigarette. The other boy gasped stumbled backward and then struggled to get up and run. But Agha was too fast. He caught his shirt from behind and with deadly efficiency ran his knife across this boy's neck also.

Tomorrow, the boy would have been seventeen. They had planned to hit the river, drink some beer, and fish. Instead, they died silently on a dirt road of Navajo Village at the hands of Agha.

He surveyed the dead and looked around for any other witnesses, wiped his knife off and calmly strolled back to the SUVs. Their families would be left to find the boys in the morning.

A short time later, the gang members fired up the SUVs, and they were moving. Three vehicles containing the Arabs were spaced a couple miles apart so as to not draw attention to the convoy. The vehicles headed out of

Navajo and to their destination, a safe house on the nearby Hopi Indian reservation.

The Hopi reservation is a Native American reservation for the Hopi and Arizona Tewa people in northeastern Arizona. It is completely surrounded by the Navajo Nation, and is very small in comparison, with an approximate population of six thousand people.

Hopi is divided into a system of villages, situated around three mesas in pueblo style. The Hopi still observe traditional religious practices, involving kivas, or rooms designed for worship, and *kachinas*, or spirit beings.

The spirit beings were restless on this night. In the Hopi's over nine-hundred-year old existence, the danger within its borders had never been this great. It now housed some of the most dangerous terrorists to ever set foot in America.

Begay arranged the housing for the Arabs. He had secretly gotten word to Agha via a courier that they would be headed to another safe house on the Hopi reservation. From there, the Arabs would go to Gallup to await their travel to the border as soon as possible. Agha smiled, knowing he would soon be on the move.

Later that evening, Agha and the Arabs arrived safely in Hopi. They entered another small safe house and into another cold, lifeless basement. Again, they waited.

All that night, Agha dreamed about that moment that he would release the weapon upon the Americans. That would be the time when his dad rose up from that field, alive again, and fighting.

In Navajo very early that morning, the usually peaceful silence of the village was shattered by the whipping rotors of flying helicopters overhead, and by scores of FBI and SWAT officers who descended in teams holding firearms and megaphones. The agents shouted orders to the locals to remain in their homes. The agents systematically went from house to house and banged on doors.

Several residents went outside before the agents got to their homes to see what was happening. The agents angrily ordered them back inside. When residents didn't readily open their doors, they kicked them down, causing extensive property damage. Small children cried, huddled in their mother's arms. Young Native American men shouted obscenities at the agents. Several were arrested. It was chaos.

Over the course of the next twenty-four hours, the FBI and SWAT officers forcefully entered homes. They overturned beds and went through closets and basements. The agents detained several innocent residents for resisting the searches. They broke into outbuildings and trailers, destroyed walls and structures, beat citizens, and committed a myriad of civil rights violations. It was all in an attempt, at all costs, to find the terrorists.

The worst incident occurred when a proud young Navajo man refused to submit to a pat down search. He had been drinking the night before and was on his way to work. After seeing what was happening to his home and people, he became angry. When he defied the agents, they knocked him down and hit him in the face with a baton. He struggled to his feet and lunged, so an FBI Agent shot him in the upper chest, taking his life in short gasps and pleading breaths.

Navajo residents looked on in horror. There was no good explanation for the killing. There was utterly no explanation for the way that law enforcement conducted itself during the raid.

The worst part was that the FBI had tipped all of the cable networks and news stations, in the hopes that they would make a big splash capturing the Arabs in dramatic fashion. Instead, several reporters had videoed the killing of the Navajo Indian.

The FBI wasn't releasing details to the media so the public was ignorant to the ongoing search for the terrorists. The stations would replay the intimate footage over and over again, provoking national outrage.

The reporters found the two nearly-decapitated Native Americans before the FBI agents had seen them. The media partially obscured the horrific neck slashes when they were shown repeatedly over the next several days. A professional had caused these cuts. The FBI's incompetence was heightened with this discovery, as they now knew that the Arabs had been there, but where they were now was anyone's guess. Time was running short.

In the aftermath of it all, Spencer dialed her cell phone and reached SAC Bowman. "They aren't here. Dammit Harold! They aren't here! The press is all over us. This is a disaster! I don't know what the hell happened. We have looked everywhere, everywhere! I don't know what to do but we are running out of time. I've got the media all over me, and this isn't good Harold! This isn't good at all. We have casualties. They were here!"

"Ok, Maria. Calm down. I hear you. I'm not happy at all either about this. But we're regrouping. We have intel coming in on the Arabs moving, possibly to Hopi. I can't tell you they are there for sure, but I think it's a good possibility. I've been in touch with the director and the White House, and the orders have been given for us to implement Operation Lockdown. You have my full backing to pull out of Navajo and immediately proceed with Operation Lockdown in Hopi. We have agent's enroute as we speak. We need all SWAT to proceed to Hopi immediately. Is that understood?"

Operation Lockdown?

Spencer knew that Operation Lockdown was a scenario that had been discussed, and sometimes "war gamed" at FBI headquarters, but no one had ever really believed it would be implemented. Until now.

The concept was simple and brutal: the United States by its military, police and whatever other resources would lock down and blockade a territory in Indian country, with armed guards blocking all entry ways, allowing no one to enter or leave, until every house in the territory was searched.

Residents who resisted would be held in detention camps across the southwest that were kept largely secret, but were real, and staffed by military guards.

The purpose of the blockade and searches was to find any terrorist presence.

The operation would only be ordered in the worst of circumstances, and when it was, normal rules were essentially ignored and martial law was put in place.

"Harold, I will report immediately. Are you sure Lockdown has been approved? What are my orders when we get to Hopi?"

He replied, "Full approval. Your orders are to find the terrorists. Detain or kill. Period."

As the FBI began moving all available assets and men to Hopi, Begay embraced Agha. His Jihadists looked on with anticipation.

Inside the safe house, Agha smiled, patted Begay on the back, and told him that the time was drawing nigh to start the attack. The three *La Raza* gang members assigned to watch Agha and the jihadists stared lifelessly at the ceiling, their throats having been ripped apart moments earlier by the jihadists. Blood trickled out of the cuts. Their eyes showed nothing but death. Begay nodded and made clear that time was of the essence.

In a small clearing not far away, several men lay pressed to the earth, their bodies covered in camouflage and face paint. No one moved. Their arms and legs seemed to mold to the earth as they trained their night vision goggles upon the house where the Arabs were pacing back and forth. From above, they looked like part of the landscape. Even the occasional bird flying overhead seemed oblivious to their presence. There was no moonlight, but the night vision specs penetrated the intense darkness and showed the dog soldiers each Arab.

"It would be an easy shot from here through the window with our rifles, but we wouldn't get them all at once", Isha thought to himself. *And we wouldn't learn any more about their plot. We need some of them alive.*

Looking to his right, he signaled to Thunder Hawk and Asija.

Isha gave a hand signal and the group began to move forward, inch by inch, stealthily, on their bellies. They crawled like snakes ever so slowly over small rocks and brush. Crickets chirped, and the wind blew, but the dog soldiers made no sound as they drew closer and closer to the house. Previously, they had gathered visual intel on the house. They knew all of the entrance and exit points and escape routes. The plan was to snatch the Arabs, without having to kill any of them, and to take them to another site for interrogation about the planned attack.

As they closed to within ten feet to the south side of the house, Isha raised his hand slightly to signal the halt. Their next act was to close in, seal the exits, and draw on the unsuspecting Arabs before they realized anything was happening. It was all going smoothly until the helicopters overhead broke the silence.

The whoosh, whoosh, whoosh, of the rotor blades startled the Arabs. They flinched and ducked down below the window. Isha tensed, and signaled for the Dog Soldiers to roll and fan out to achieve a fire angle on the Arabs. Seconds later, all hell broke loose.

The front door flung open. Agha burst through it at a dead run to the SUV approximately fifty yards down the road. Isha watched and raised his rifle, locking the man's head in his scope. The shot wasn't a clear one.

I can't blow our cover and lose this opportunity.

Isha made the split second decision not to fire. He kept his scope trained on the man as he ran.

In his peripheral vision, Isha saw movement. His eye released from his scope, and his head turned to the right.

More Arabs sprinted from the house and to getaway cars. He raised his hand in a gesture for the Dog Soldiers to stand down. They watched and counted as all of the Jihadists exited the house at a dead run and boarded the SUVs. None of the Dog Soldiers could move or breathe as they watched their prey speed away with Officer Roland Begay.

The Dog Soldiers got up and went inside the home to look for any evidence. Isha saw the dead *La Raza* gang members. He searched them. They had no significant information. He took note of the manner in which they were cut. Isha found a slip of paper on the floor of the house with a name and a phone number. The number was local to New Mexico, 575, area code. He pocketed it, and his team ran out the door.

CHAPTER 14

Operation Lockdown, in the end, was a disaster. Scores of heavily armed agents descended upon Hopi Land. The entry and exit points to the reservation had all been locked down, and no resident was allowed to enter or leave. Barriers were set up and checkpoints were erected at each entry and exit point. FBI agents detained and arrested a family that had an important medical appointment outside of Hopi when they refused to comply with commands to stop at the checkpoint. Agents forcefully entered homes, broke doors, searched rooms and destroyed items, including sacred *kachina* carvings, only to wind up empty handed.

One elderly Hopi grandmother, Mansi, was in the middle of making some *Poovol piki*, one of her favorite dishes, when three black-clad agents stormed into her home with guns drawn. She jumped at the sound, spilling her corn meal on the floor.

She involuntarily shuddered as the agents yelled and screamed at her. "Get down, get down!"

Mansi started to squat down but wasn't quick enough and was thrown to the floor on top of the corn meal, breaking her left wrist in a sickening crunch. She cried out in pain as agents threw chairs and furniture around, and overturned anything that might contain a secret hiding place. She cried when she looked up to see her *Kachinas* broken into pieces on the floor of her living room. One of the *Kachinas*, *He-e-wuhti*, was over fifty years old and a gift from her grandmother. Its dark warrior face was severed from its body, and was staring at her sideways as the agents stepped over it, and out the door, saying nothing.

Other Hopi could only watch in horror as the agents upended and ransacked their peaceful lives and homes. They had not asked for the Arabs to come.

The agents did not find any of the Arabs.

By the end of the search, government authorities had herded a group of Hopis who had resisted onto a bus. The bus was now on its way out of the reservation and to a detention camp. There, the Hopi people would be detained for an indefinite period and interrogated about their knowledge, if any, of the Arabs. Centuries of discontent, shock and sadness were etched on their faces as the bus carrying them rolled away. The news cameras and their opportunistic operators once again filmed select shots of the barricades and the horrified faces of the Hopi.

Spencer was furious. Her case and reputation were both unraveling. She went into her phone and found the number for her contact in Navajo, Criminal Investigator Joe Eagle.

"Joe, I need to see you right away. We have a serious problem, and I need your immediate help."

"Whoa, whoa. Ok, is this Agent Spencer? What's going on? I am kind of tied up on my own things out here."

"This is literally a life and death matter, and if you won't voluntarily meet me, I will have the judge subpoena you as a material witness. How is that? Refusing isn't an option, Joe!"

"Wow, no need to get hostile. Where would you like to meet?"

"Gallup. Meet me at the FBI Office there. I'll be there within an hour."

"Ok. I'll see you there."

Joe hung up and thought about his options. He had been in this position before with the FBI and he knew that he was in a position of possible danger. He would be ok, but he needed a plan. Normally Maria Spencer was composed and helpful. This was not like her.

At a table inside the Gallup FBI field office, Spencer sat impatiently and checked her phone repeatedly. Then, Joe suddenly entered the room. Spencer rose.

"Hello, Joe. Thank you for coming."

"Hi, Agent Spencer. No problem. I'm happy to help. Although some people from your agency don't seem to like me," Joe chuckled.

She tensed. "Well, I don't need your help. I'm running an investigation that has White House backing and is the highest priority in the FBI. What I need Joe, is for you to tell me what you have found in leads on the Arabs in Navajo. Now."

"Why don't we sit down, as a starter?" Joe smiled, attempting to calm the situation.

She took a seat first. Joe thought she didn't look as good as usual. She was stressed out and tense. She also looked tired.

"Agent Spencer, I will not talk about anything unless we first have an understanding. I will not give up any of my sources. And your guys at the Bureau back off and let me do my job."

"Ok. That's fine, Joe. We don't have a lot of time. I need to know everything you have learned about the whereabouts of the Arabs. We are running out of time. I'm sure you're privy to the details of the searches of Navajo and Hopi."

"Yes, I am. In fact, the whole reservation is aware. If the Arabs were still in either Navajo or Hopi, I can assure you that they would have been given up. The people do not want them there. But I do not believe many of the people will talk to you now. You have destroyed their trust, again."

"I'm not concerned about their trust! I care about finding terrorists who are in our country about to un-leash terror attacks! I need to hear what you know, and I need it now!" Spencer's face was red with emotion.

"Agent Spencer," Joe was speaking slowly and calm-ly, "I have a lot of information. Including a drug arrest involving a man named Daniel Thunder Hawk, which you know about. That arrest was connected to a cartel, which has been transporting drugs and people into our home-land. I learned that the Arabs were likely there in Navajo. While I was searching for them, Thunder Hawk was captured by the cartel. I followed leads and found a scene by the San Juan River in Farmington, where all the cartel members had been killed, and Thunder Hawk was missing, most likely taken by ..."

"Who killed them? Who killed the cartel people?"

"Agent, I have some information on the killings but need some more time to develop it. I don't know for sure but have an idea."

"What's your idea? Who are they? I need to speak with them right away! This is the first I have learned about this. How long have you had this information?"

Joe smiled. "As do I, Agent. And we will. If we are right, they will pass along information to us. We have known of this for some time, and are still looking. They are secretive and will only deal with those they choose."

"No, Mr. Eagle! Stop the secretive bullshit! Your work is through. I need the contact for whoever these people are, and I need it immediately. You've already obstructed this investigation. These people, whoever they are, may possess the final critical information that is needed. I'm quite sure that you don't want to obstruct a federal investigation, not the least of which is a federal investigation that involves national security. Do you realize that I can order you detained?! Now, I need this name and information now!"

Joe sat in silence and stared defiantly at the agent. He had looked death in the face before and survived it.

Her threat was not something that he feared.

"This meeting is ended," Joe rose.

Spencer stood and pulled her firearm and pointed it directly at him. The tension was palpable. Her face reflected confusion and fear.

"Sit down, Mr. Eagle! Now."

Joe stood calmly.

At the moment of maximum intensity, Joe gently put his hand up and then sat back slowly into his chair. He smiled very subtly and raised his hands in a show of peace.

She pointed the gun at him for a few seconds longer, lowered it, and then holstered the gun.

"Agent, I give you my word that I will not leave until this matter is resolved. No need for the gun." Joe's voice now radiated calmness, like his grandmother's soft and kind reassurance. He had forced his mind into a meditative state again.

Spencer nodded her head.

"I just need the name, Joe." Spencer replied as she was dialing her supervisor, SAC Bowman.

"Harold, I may need authority to arrest a Navajo Nation Criminal Investigator. Yes. Yes. I do believe that he has obstructed my investigation." Spencer nodded into the phone. A few moments later she appeared to come to a conclusion, and turned her attention back to Joe Eagle.

"Ok, thank you. As of now you are under arrest until I get the information that I need. You are not free to leave, Mr. Eagle."

Joe spoke again, even more calmly than before.

"Agent, so far the efforts of the FBI have not been productive. You would agree, no? We are all rowing the same direction. I want to find the Arabs as much as you do. These men, these Dog Soldiers, if I am correct about them, are elite warriors, and they know how to accomplish the mission. If they do not want to speak with you, my giving you their names will not accomplish anything. You will never find them unless they want to be found, and then we'd lose our connection to them, and with that loss, any leads they have on the Arabs. You can arrest me, and I will sit in a cell while the Arabs prepare, but if you want to find these men, you must let me communicate with them and let me help you find them."

Spencer sat silently and pondered her options. There was a calm wisdom in Eagle's voice, and, so far, nothing had worked for her. Eagle's mannerism made her feel almost at ease, which she thought was odd. She made her decision quickly.

"Ok, Joe; but we need this information. I am sure you understand that. I will give you my personal cell number. I ask that you get on this right away, and call me as soon as you hear anything."

"You have my word, Agent."

"You are free to leave." Spencer stated smugly.

Joe stared at her and then smiled. "Thank you, Agent. I appreciate that," he snarked.

Spencer, realizing that her last comment had been insensitive, responded in kind "I'm sorry, Joe, I am looking forward to working with you."

As Joe got into his car he breathed audibly and slowly. He dialed Wendell, the medicine man.

"I saw them. I know that they have come." Joe was speaking rapidly.

"Yes, I know Joe. Slow down just a bit." The medicine man laughed.

"The leader's name is Isha. He will be in contact with us soon. He believes that the government and others will be watching very closely, so he has asked me to relay some information to you. It is a code that the Dog Soldiers use. Keep it safe. If you need Isha, call me anytime, son."

"Okay, thank you," Joe said. "I will come over to get the code."

"That will be fine, Joe. Come by the house."

"The FBI is not getting anywhere in this investigation. If we want to solve it and find the Arabs, it is up to us," Joe added. "We have to do so in a way that the FBI doesn't know anything until we tell them, so that they don't jump the gun, again."

"Joe, did you also know that Daniel is one of them now?" The medicine man was talking in a softer voice.

"One of them? You mean a Dog Soldier?"

He had not seen Thunder Hawk since the scene in Farmington. Now he was really intrigued.

"Yes, that's right. He's coming back to the Navajo Nation and he'll be our contact."

Joe processed all this new information. *Daniel Thunder Hawk? A Dog Soldier?* "Ok. What happens next?"

"Thunder Hawk will call," Wendell said.

Joe hung up somewhat stunned by the news, but happy that Thunder Hawk was ok.

Now that the hunt for the Arabs and the cartel was on, Joe was actually relieved to have Thunder Hawk back, and on his side. He sped off to the medicine man's house to obtain the codes.

CHAPTER 15

Joe was leaving a café in Window Rock when he received a partially coded message. It was from Thunder Hawk. Joe understood it using the code. The message was short and to the point, but plain as day.

There are numerous targets on the way to Gallup. Identified associate meeting there now.

Joe texted back. Is this who I think it is?
Thunder Hawk replied. Yes, come right away.
Joe turned for Gallup.

Meanwhile, Spencer was leaving the situation room in the Albuquerque FBI Office. SAC Bowman had told her an hour earlier that headquarters was taking over "her" case, that she had lost focus, caused untold damage to the reputation of the FBI, and possibly cost human lives.

"The raids of the Navajo Nation and Hopi reservation had been complete failures," Bowman explained. "You are off the case."

Bowman was blaming Spencer to cover his ass.

This was a career ender. The FBI never stood for loss of its reputation, no matter what. This was "it" also for Maria Spencer.

As she exited the room, her anger reached a boiling point. *Reputation of the FBI! I built this case! We wouldn't be anywhere without my work!* She silently thought to herself.

She thought over the countless days and nights spent poring over case files and data, connecting the dots on what appeared to be seemingly random drug cases, wiretap applications, and her debriefing Arabs, all to get to *what*? This?

No, this can't be the end for me!

She now believed that it was the FBI that had lost focus. It was not unusual at all for targets, such as Bashir, to lie about aspects of an operation.

She had no doubt he had lied to her about details during her debrief. For heaven's sake, he had tried to kill her; no doubt he would lie to her. Spencer knew that she had one hope to complete this case and to save her career: she had to find the Arabs.

Joe answered his phone: "This is Eagle."

"Joe, this is Agent Spencer." Her voice sounded urgent.

"Hello, Agent. How can I help you?"

"I need your help locating the Arabs. It is critical and a matter of national security. I apologize for what happened earlier. I think we can and should work together. I can help with resources."

Joe paused for a moment. "Agent, I think we can accomplish more working together than apart." Joe hesitated and then continued. "I don't want the FBI at large to know what I am about to tell you. I am on my way to Gallup. I have reason to believe that the Arabs are located there. Can you bring a tracker so that we can follow them if they leave Gallup?"

Spencer's voice now carried an air of excitement to it.

"Of course, thank you, Joe. Thank you. I will bring a few trackers, and if you need anything else, please do not hesitate. Where will we meet in Gallup?"

"Not sure yet. We'll let you know."

Spencer was running as fast as her heels would allow through the halls of the FBI building.

SAC Bowman looked up in interest, as well as concern. He lifted the phone and contacted his deputy, and asked that a detail be assigned to Special Agent Maria Spencer.

Spencer was on the fly when she hit the door and made it to her car in record time. As she was opening her door, she

realized she had forgotten the tracking devices.

"Shit!"

Knowing that the FBI keeps a log of use of the devices, she knew that she couldn't "officially" log out any of the equipment. For the first time in her career, she was about to make a series of moves that could cost her the title of Special Agent. Without those maneuvers, her career was essentially over, anyway. Between the times that devices were checked in after use, there was a delay in processing.

She had just handled a smaller drug case and returned the tracker back into the bin.

She thought *"That may work."*

Spencer casually turned and walked back through the doors, strolled past the guard and headed towards the evidence area. As she neared the door, SAC Bowman was rounding the corner at the end of the hall. She leaped through the door into the evidence room moments before Bowman looked up.

As she'd surmised, her tracker hadn't been picked up yet. She put the device in her purse, held her breath and waited while Bowman kept pacing down the hall towards her location. His cell phone rang.

"Sure, sure, yes I will get that. It's in my office. I'm heading that way now."

Bowman turned and Spencer heard him heading the opposite direction down the hall. As soon as his footsteps faded, she raced out of the room and down the hall towards the exit door again.

While cameras watched the evidence room, it would be unlikely anyone would pick up on her grabbing the tracking device, and even if they did, Spencer hoped her plan would be in full motion, and that "they" would understand later why she did what she did.

Seconds later, she was in her car, and off, headed towards Gallup.

Isha and his band of Dog Soldiers were in place, forming around the perimeter of the Red Lion Hotel in Gallup, New Mexico. Isha had already learned the name of the man who had taken the Arabs there: Officer Begay with Navajo Nation Narcotics, who had knowledge of the area.

Through other technology, Isha identified the location of a safe house that was tied to Begay in Gallup. It didn't take them long to again locate the dark SUVs that they'd seen in Hopi. They had not moved. There was no doubt that the Arabs were here in Gallup.

The Dog Soldiers believed there were around seventeen or eighteen Arabs, including the dark one who had run out of the safe house first.

They would have to move with speed and force and not make any mistakes to capture them. That was their first goal. If some had to be killed to accomplish that goal, so be it, but Isha had instructed his men that the first goal was to capture.

They all knew that the intelligence they would gain from torturing the Arabs would be critical to stop the planned attack. Then, if they had to kill them, it was a matter of business.

Isha spoke quietly into their closed circuit radios. The coded language disguised their communications. The other Dog Soldiers lay motionless at various points surrounding the hotel. Isha let them know that they would wait until there was movement. Each man had water and provisions.

The Dog Soldiers were camouflaged and prepared to wait out the Arabs as long as it took.

Following Isha's prior orders, Thunder Hawk sent another coded message to Joe. He told him the package was at the Red Lion Hotel, but not to approach except at night, and on foot, and only when Isha said it was safe to do so. Joe quickly acknowledged that he understood.

Joe called Spencer.

"Yes, Joe. Have you found them?" Her urgency was back.

"Agent Spencer, we have information to believe that the Arabs are at the Red Lion Hotel in Gallup, but we have been told to only approach when instructed to do so, and only when it is dark. ..." Joe paused because he thought he heard a familiar sound on his phone.

Agent Spencer closed her phone and gunned her government issued vehicle. She put her flashers on and was flying westbound on Interstate 40.

"Agent? Agent! Oh Shit!" Joe slammed his closed fist against the dash of the car. "Son of a bitch."

Joe punched his accelerator and reached one hundred miles per hour quickly as they headed southbound towards Interstate 40 and then to Gallup. Unless they got there first, this FBI Agent might blow the entire thing, and worse yet, get Dog Soldiers and innocent civilians killed.

Agha ordered lights out in the hotel room, with the exception of small flashlights. None of his killers spoke. Officer Begay had not yet returned. He would be back within the next two hours. Agha called El Tiburón.

They were leaving for the border of Mexico, as it was no longer safe to stay in the interior of this country. Allah willing, within six hours they would be with El Tiburón, and would acquire the weapon that would make the Americans forever remember the error of their ways.

Agha peeled back the blinds. He scanned the parking lot and saw nothing out of the ordinary. The American FBI and all of its supposed power had been no match for the Arabs. At every juncture they had been too slow.

Bureaucrats.

Agha marveled at their good fortune and knew that Allah was watching out for them.

As he moved his hands down to let the blinds close, he saw movement in the parking lot. A dark, official-looking car screeched its tires, throwing up gravel as it roared to a stop.

He opened the blinds wider and saw a woman get out of the car. By the look of the car and her demeanor she was clearly law enforcement. Agha motioned to the Arabs, who all tensed. He dialed Begay. The time to move was now.

"I'm on my way." Begay hung up on the other end.

As Agha continued to watch, the female walked toward the door of the hotel.

If she knows about us, this woman could blow up everything.

Agha had to assume the worst. He made a quick decision and directed the group to get ready to move and to split in half. Half would go with him, and the rest would leave a few minutes later with Begay.

Agha and his group slinked out of the room and into the hallway, headed for the staircase and down to the lobby.

At about the same time, Isha and his men also saw Spencer arrive.

Isha thought, "*Shit this is bad.*"

He got on the radio to his men, rapidly formulating a plan to stop her from entering the hotel.

If she goes in, she could eliminate any surprise. We have to put her down.

Isha instructed Asija to ready a dart, which the Dog Soldiers had pre-laced with a powerful sedative. Asija did so without hesitation. On orders from Isha, he prepared to fire, but the agent ducked below one of the dark SUVs. She appeared to be touching something under the car. There was no shot, and Isha barked orders for him to wait. The agent lingered for a moment, and then crawled further under the SUV.

Unbeknownst to Isha and the Dog Soldiers, Spencer was placing a tracking device under the vehicle.

She slid out from under the SUV. Isha again signaled Asija to shoot. Just as the agent was almost clear from under the SUV, movement distracted everyone including Isha. His blood ran cold.

Shadowy figures seemed to be everywhere. Hurtling out of the hotel and running right at her. She did not see them coming.

No way she can escape in time.

Isha now saw one of the Arabs drop. Asija had fired. All hell was breaking loose.

The one in front, Isha had seen before. The dark one, the leader.

They were on top of the agent now, pinning her to the ground. She struggled as Isha raised his rifle. He didn't have a clear shot on the dark one. Too close to the agent.

Isha turned, aimed at the second Arab and fired, blowing the side of his head off. The dark one slammed his gun into the side of the agent's head. Isha watched her go limp. The Arabs were jumping into the car and pulling her inside.

Something fell from the agent's hand and out the door, as the leader revved the engine and slammed it into reverse. They screamed out of the parking lot.

Isha was on the move and calling out to his fellow soldiers to get to the SUV. As they ran in that direction, a car screamed to a stop twenty-five yards away. Joe leaped out, yelling to Isha.

"It's me! Don't shoot!" Joe held his hands in the air.

Isha motioned Joe over to the rear of the hotel to take a position near the other exit.

Seconds later, another vehicle sped away from that side of the hotel. A Dog Soldier on that side caught a plate number. Isha already knew. Officer Begay. He looked at his men who watched the rear of the car as it faded into the distance. The Arabs had all escaped, past the gauntlet of Dog Soldiers.

The hotel clerks ran outside.

The authorities have got to be en route.

Isha signaled his men and jogged over to where he had seen the object fall from the SUV from Agent Spencer's hand. It was her cell phone. As Isha picked it up, Joe stated: "Luck is with us Isha. That is our tracker phone. It must have fallen when the Arabs grabbed her." Isha looked down at the cell phone. An audible ping was going off. The tracking device was engaged. "She placed the tracker also. We've got them Isha." Joe patted Isha's shoulder. Isha acknowledged Joe and said a silent prayer of thanks.

On the ground, one Arab lay still, unconscious from the powerful sedative contained within the dart. The other Arab was dead. Isha told Joe to handcuff the live one and take him to a secure place, and that he would get in touch with him about the Arabs very soon. Joe said that he would take him over to the Gallup police, to put him in the custody of a friend, until the man could be turned over to the feds. Joe promised that he would get back in touch with Isha.

Isha rounded up his team of Dog Soldiers. Joe turned away and handcuffed the sedated Arab. When he looked back up there was only darkness. The Dog Soldiers had already vanished.

CHAPTER 16

The Arabs bound and gagged Spencer and threw her in the back seat of the SUV. She was waking now. They were midway to Grants, New Mexico.

As Spencer looked around her and noticed the men with vacant, dead eyes, staring forward, expressionless. She went wide-eyed. She moved and felt the ropes. Fear gripped her. She panicked, wriggling and struggling at the ropes that bound her hands. Agha turned and stared at her. Spencer looked back with anger, trying to hide her fear. Agha clenched his teeth. He motioned to the jihadist next to her who forcefully grabbed her arms and put a hood over her head.

Agha pushed the SUV a little faster. He pulled his knife and held it at his side. Spencer's chest heaved from the adrenaline rush.

Agha looked down at the map that Begay had drawn for him to reach *El Malpais*.

El Malpais National Conservation Area is a national park in New Mexico. Over millions of years, volcanic eruptions spewed out molten lava creating dramatic sandstone cliffs, canyons, cinder cones, caves, and other eerie formations.

The lava flows made the terrain black, pockmarked. Pueblo Indians from Zuni, Acoma, and Laguna pueblos had long lived in the area. It was a sacred area to some people, and to others, it was a fascinating destination.

The National Park Service had recently closed all of the caves and restricted them from public entrance because a fungus was killing millions of bats that made the caves their home.

Due to the closings, Begay believed this would be the perfect place for the Arabs to wait. There would be little public presence. New Mexico State Road 53, which turned south off I-40 just east of Grants, would be safer than the major highways.

From here, they would connect with State Road 180, head through Reserve and into Deming, New Mexico, then over to Las Cruces and ultimately near Sunland Park they would sneak across the International Border and unite with El Tiburón.

He communicated with Agha by text and was now waiting for the Arab's arrival, but first, Agha would deal with the female agent.

As he reached the exit for Road 53, his satellite telephone beeped. He looked back and saw Spencer looking directly at him, with defiance in her face. She was still, but breathing heavily.

Agha's phone rang, and he answered it.

"We are headed north as you told us to Denver. Where are you?" Begay asked.

"We're almost to the cave. I'm glad you made it out safely. Stay the course, and let me know when you get there."

Agha breathed a sigh of relief and looked in his rear view mirror. The jihadists with him were darkly clad and heavily armed. They carried weapons of various types, AR-15 rifles, .45 pistols, and lethal combat knives, which were now at the ready. Their eyes betrayed little emotion, and save for an occasional cough, the group could be apparitions, deadly black clad ghosts who would soon unleash havoc on unsuspecting citizens.

"Yes, we will let you know when we make it." Begay hung up.

Agha was pleased.

As he hung up and turned around, Spencer lurched forward and violently head butted the man next to her in the jaw. She tried to kick in the other direction and strike the other jihadist. That man reacted immediately, dodging and knocking her leg to the side. He then grabbed her by the shoulders. Whipping her around quickly he put his arms around her neck and choked her until she stopped struggling.

Agha reached into a bag in the passenger seat and pulled out a syringe that was filled with clear fluid. He squeezed the bottom and released a small volume. Spencer was breathing and almost unconscious from the chokehold. Agha handed the syringe to the jihadist behind him. Spencer tried to struggle again. The jihadist plunged the syringe into Spencer's leg and she groaned and stopped struggling.

Joe was on his way to Grants. The cell phone GPS kept a steady "ping" on the SUV as it tracked Spencer and the Arabs. The SUV turned south at State Road 53.

Joe contacted Thunder Hawk. "Looks like they are taking the back roads, you think, Daniel? What's down that way?" he asked.

"That leads down towards the Zuni Pueblo, El Morro monument, and *El Malpais* State Park. Not much else but roads. He could keep going and make it to Deming from Road 117, and then pretty easily to the Mexican border. Keep a low profile and it wouldn't be hard. That tracker is working." Thunder Hawk continued: "Reserve is on the road and Deming, but I bet they will stop in *El Malpais* somewhere. It's really easy to hide down there."

Joe agreed. "I think that you're right, Daniel. Let's keep a distance and keep an eye out for the other vehicle."

Ahead of them by five minutes, Agha and the other Arabs with him had just made their turn to head south on 53.

He pulled to a stop at Junction Cave, in the El Calderon area of *El Malpais*, about twenty minutes south of Grants.

Junction Cave was created over one-hundred-thousand years by lava flow from the *El Calderon* (cinder cones).

The cave is said to be wild, with no lights or pathways within it. Just past the entrance to the cave is the "twilight zone," where there is extreme darkness, with only hints of light from the cave opening.

It was in the twilight zone that Agha first turned on his small lantern. Spencer hung loosely over his shoulder. She was still unconscious from the sedative Agha had administered.

Suspended from the ceiling, upside down were numerous sinister looking bats, hanging there, oblivious to the two human figures below them.

Agha moved the lantern around from side to side, but the dark walls of the cave didn't appear to have any other lurking creatures.

He walked forward farther into the cavern and the jihadists followed. He pulled Agent Spencer forward off his shoulder and propped her on the cavern floor, against a wall. He set his lantern down adjacent to the wall. He picked up Agent Spencer and pushed her hard against the wall. Her head slumped against her shoulder. Agha pushed it upright and then let it fall to the side. Her hands were still bound.

He lit a cigarette and puffed slightly, then walked back towards the opening and looked out at the night sky. It was fitting that tonight was a full moon.

A few bats fluttered through the sky, but otherwise the night was silent. Agha pulled his dark hood over his head.

Tonight, we will get what we can out of the American agent. Then we will kill her and dump her body in the cave.

Before anyone could find her, Agha planned to have unleashed the weapon and to become a martyr, along with his fellow warriors. Then nothing else would matter, including the death of this agent. Praise Allah, nothing could stop them now.

Agha turned and went back inside. Greater darkness descended upon Agha and all of his jihadists inside the cave. A couple of the men lit flashlights. The bats looked down on them in stoic silence.

Across the cave now Agha saw that the agent was stirring slightly. Her head moved forward, and her arms moved slightly as she was waking up. One of the men trained his flashlight directly into the agent's face. Agha moved forward and to the side, about five feet away. Another moved the lantern closer to Agha.

Spencer opened her eyes. As she was waking, in her haziness, she saw her worst nightmare. Adrenaline raced through her body. She began struggling with her whole being against the ropes that bound her. Spencer's arms wouldn't move well and neither would her legs. She could not speak. A shadowy figure was moving in front of her, and her eyes opened as wide as they would go.

Terror gripped her. It was the dark Arab and around him were numerous other dark figures.

Where am I?

Spencer struggled to slow her heart rate. She forced herself to think through the situation. *Is this a cave?*

Her brain raced. She looked to the ceiling. Through the beam of lantern light she saw the bats.

I'm in a cave. Think.

Spencer tried to calm down and slow her breathing, despite knowing that without help coming, the arabas would undoubtedly kill her. She realized her life might end here in this dark hole, surrounded by prehistoric looking creatures, at the hands of these ghosts.

Breathe. Calm down. Think.

Spencer was losing the battle to control her breathing, and she began to hyperventilate. She thought she might pass out, as the dark Arab reached forward and pulled her gag down. She gasped for air. She looked down and coughed several times, trying to breathe. The man put his hand under her chin and raised it.

"You are in a cave. I am sure you have already figured that out. I told you when we were driving that you would give us the information that we need. You will tell us how to avoid being seen as we head to the border. If you at any time lie to me, we will kill you, but first we may have some fun." Agha smiled a dark, sinister, sickening smile.

Spencer tried to channel her training and calm herself before she spoke.

Suddenly, bats flew out of the cave, disrupting her thought process.

"You all are animals!" Spencer shouted.

Agha laughed. "Well, well, welcome to our little gathering."

"Where am I? Where is this cave?" She yelled.

"There's no need for you to know your location, and no one is going to hear you. So you can talk as loud as you want. It won't help. It is doubtful you will leave here tonight. No one will know, for a long, long time."

Spencer panted, feeling a panic attack coming on. She had been in panic situations before, in training with the FBI and in situations in the field.

She had also hit "the wall" before in her marathons and knew how to fight through a bad situation, but this was worse, way worse. She forced herself to focus on her breathing. Her breathing and heart rate began to slow.

When she was able to calm down after a short period, her mind told her to talk. She would try to survive however she could. "I'll tell you."

Agha again smiled. "Where are your drones? Are they looking for us?"

Spencer thought quickly and said: "They will be near El Paso. They will be looking for the SUVs," Spencer lied.

Agha did not know, nor would Spencer tell him, that the federal government was actively, right now, utilizing its newest and most sensitive "camera" to locate the Arabs.

The ARGUS system, installed in a drone, could stream 1.8 billion pixels of resolution from 17,500 feet. In those images, you can clearly see a bird in flight and people walking in any given area, "live," so that it is even possible to go back several days to where it was "looking" to see what was happening back then.

Most of the components of ARGUS were top secret, and Spencer did not know how the system worked, but she did know that it was just a matter of time before the group of jihadists would be detected. If she could figure her location, she could somehow alert her colleagues where to "look."

Agha spoke again, this time much more harshly. "I told you that if you ever lied to me I would kill you."

Agha leaned forward and drew a long knife from his waist-band. He felt the blade a few times, looked up at Spencer, and in a flash moved it to the front of her neck.

She moved backwards, and hit her head on the cavern wall. She felt the knife start cutting into her neck slightly and saw the intense look of hate in Agha's eyes.

The next thing that she saw did not register at all. It made no sense. As if in a dream, one of the Arabs suddenly flew sideways and hit the cavern wall with a heavy thud. Things were in slow motion now.

Was that an arrow?

Spencer saw an arrow protruding through his head. The arrow point rested against the cavern wall.

What the hell?

She turned fully towards the falling Arab, as he slumped to the ground, the arrow scraped down the wall like nails on a chalkboard.

That sound provided an eerie opening to the hell that had broken loose within the cavern.

CHAPTER 17

Suddenly, the cavern exploded in turmoil. Bodies moved in every direction. Dust kicked up from the bottom of the cave. Rocks tumbled forward and banged against the cave walls.

شباح! (Ghosts!) the jihadists yelled.

Agha turned abruptly, peering through the darkness, long-bladed knife in hand intent on confronting the ensuing danger.

As he turned, Agha saw another arrow whiz through the air and strike the neck of one of his men. The arrow severed the windpipe of his comrade with a sickening thump. The man fell to the ground gasping. He was one of Agha's most trusted soldiers.

He watched the soldier clutch his throat and claw feverishly at the arrow as he sunk to the cavern floor, and to whatever was awaiting him in his next life.

Agha and his other warriors moved faster, sensing the danger that they confronted. Agha's heart pounded inside of him.

Meanwhile, Isha and his Dog Soldiers moved forward at lightning speed. Like shadows and wraiths, they fought with dexterity and efficiency. The Dog Soldiers darted, danced, circled, and dodged, moving to the sides of the Arabs.

To Maria it appeared that the Arabs waded through molasses, while the Dog Soldiers flew on pockets of air as they positioned themselves into attack range around the cavern.

The Jihadists' lives flashed before their eyes. Agha struggled to make sense of the scene.

Leaping into the middle of the Arabs, Isha, suddenly made a long sideways swipe with his knife. The knife slashed completely through the side of the neck and carotid artery of one of the older Arabs.

A guttural yip erupted from Isha's mouth as he threw his head back and screamed at having drawn first blood. The animal sound reverberated around the cavern, frightening Spencer. She ducked her head and tried to move backwards and disappear into the cavern wall.

Bats woke from their slumber and began to beat their wings frantically, flying without direction and then out towards the night air and away from the sounds and stench of death.

Another of the Dog Soldiers jumped up and grabbed an Arab in the air and turned him around, jerking him backwards by his hair. He grabbed him roughly from behind and plunged a knife deep into the side of his neck. As he pulled and ripped the knife forward hard, the entire side of the Arab's neck burst open with a gush of bright red blood.

In a panic, Agha watched the blood spurt and gush as the Arab fell hard and the blood pooled around him, the other Jihadists watched in horror. Sensing that they were completely outmanned, they began to dive to the ground. Visceral screams filled the air.

The Arabs looked up from the ground at the ghosts. To a man they knew they had to escape from these demons that had invaded the cavern.

Spencer looked up and watched the falling bodies and blood and shuddered at the screams.

Isha cried out again and leaped to the far right side of the cavern and directly next to another Arab who was still standing, staring in shock at the scene that was unfolding.

In one swift motion, Isha drove his knife into the liver of the Arab, who attempted to turn, too slow. In the very next moment he sliced downward, severing the tendons in the Arab's right wrist, and caused the gun in his hand to fall to the cavern floor. The Arab collapsed, clutching his side, and slumped to the floor.

His eyes rolled back into his head, and he was gone.

Isha kicked the gun aside and screamed like a banshee. It sounded like the cry of a wolf just beginning to taste the flesh of its vanquished prey.

In this moment, Isha was beginning to transport to another time. He felt it. He had tasted blood. He was now on another battlefield.

There were other Dog Soldiers beside him; from the time of his forefathers. His people were watching him. They were chanting, dancing, and waging war. Isha was slaughtering their enemies. He felt his blood coursing through his veins. Generations of his people danced around him now in the shadows around the cavern, their chants were audible. Isha heard them and began to chant with them.

As he closed his eyes, he could smell the blood, and he could see the death, and he could taste the fear in the air, which hung motionless in the room like the bats that had earlier been right above their heads, witnesses to a slaughter that had begun in another time.

The remaining Arabs hit the floor of the cavern and lay there motionless. Hands on their heads, they covered their ears from the deafening, freakish sounds coming from this wraith that danced and screamed like a demon banished from hell.

Agha slithered away from the Dog Soldiers, deeper into the cavern, around a corner and out of sight. He clutched his knife and gritted his teeth as he heard the sounds of some ancient war dance.

Isha danced around the fallen Arabs as his Dog Soldiers stood watch over the Arabs who were still alive and lying motionless, Isha danced around each of them, chanting, singing, beating his chest, and calling out to the ghosts in the night. Shadows seemed to dance around the walls, in unison with Isha. It seemed that the whole cavern had come to life.

The Dog Soldiers tied the hands of the Arabs. Eight still breathed life. One of them tried to resist, and a Dog Soldier thrust a knife into the back of his skull. The Arab flinched a few times and then went limp. The seven remaining Arabs were still, tied up next to each other.

The Dog Soldiers bound their feet together and propped each of them up on their knees, facing forward, spacing them evenly in a circle, around the interior of the cavern walls. Agha peered through the darkness from within the interior of the cave, and he could see his comrades kneeling, heads down, and facing the center of the cavernous room, as if they were about to participate in a ceremony.

Agha winced as he saw several of his soldiers lying dead on the cavern floor. He seethed, and hatred filled his soul. These people had killed his trusted warriors. He longed to avenge them now. If he leaped, Agha thought, he could kill the leader and maybe his warriors could rise up and fight off the rest. But he realized the futility of such a plan as he saw the leader begin walking around the circle, looking into the face of each of Agha's warriors.

As he watched them, Isha turned and lit a torch. The torch sparked to life casting light all around the cavern.

Agha saw the anguish and fear on his men's faces. He ducked down and inched further back into the cavern, still able to see around a corner. Another Dog Soldier walked to the center of the cavern and began laying out a circle of stones. When he finished placing the stones, a Dog Soldier came to the center and laid several sticks and a log within the circle.

Isha waved the torch back and forth rhythmically, chanting. It was an ancient warrior chant that had been handed down through generations, eventually to him.

The torch went side to side and threw shadows, which seemed to dance on the cavern walls. The words seemed to come from somewhere deep inside of Isha. The chant came from a time long ago, from men who had walked many battlefields before him. Spencer raised her head. She saw hypnotically through a haze, as if in a dream, a torch waving back and forth, back and forth. She thought she recognized the man but wasn't sure. She saw the Arabs kneeling in a circle, heads down, with other men holding knives above them. Although she saw it with her eyes, Spencer had trouble processing the whole scene. She struggled to clear her mind.

Suddenly, Joe Eagle burst into the cave and ran to the outside of the room where the Arabs were tied. Joe walked a few more steps forward and cut off his flashlight; in reverence, he stopped at the entrance to the room.

Isha stepped back and forth, back and forth, moving in a circle. Three other Dog Soldiers followed him, lock

146

step, moving and chanting around the fire. Isha threw his head back, as if it was jerked by an unseen force, and screamed out a warrior's cry. The Arabs flinched and looked down. Isha cried out with the cry of a chorus of long lost warriors, the cries of the Dog Soldiers, who were back from the grave and ready to finish this battle. The cry was long, and high pitched, and loud, and it reverberated against the walls of the cavern.

As if in a dream, Isha moved toward him like a ghost horse, and then in an instant, the torch flew forward and smashed violently into the Arab's eye. The sound was sickening as the torch crushed the eye socket and fire leaped onto the eyeball. The Arab screamed loudly in terror and pain and grabbed his eye. The white-hot heat seared his eye and he fell to the ground, screaming. Isha stood over him and continued chanting and dancing, torch raised high, this time in a low, measured voice. He looked towards another Arab who began pulling at his arms and trying to free himself. Isha turned around, then back again, circled, and screaming, pulled his knife from his belt and plunged it into the Arab's forehead. With a sickening pull, the knife came out, and the Arab fell sideways, his head nearly split in half.

One of the other Arabs began vomiting and coughing. He fell to the ground, and laid still. The Arabs who remained prayed beseeching Allah to save them from this demon.

The Dog Soldiers stopped. Isha sheathed his knife in his belt, and placed the torch on the cavern floor.

The other Dog Soldiers sat down around the fire and placed their hands in front of them in a gesture that conveyed that the battle was over and had been won.

Joe stood silent, unmoving. Spencer was unable to speak. When words came, the first person to utter them was Isha.

He walked forward to the four remaining Arabs and told them to stand. The Arabs hesitated, not knowing what this meant. A Dog Soldier abruptly stood up and jerked an Arab to his feet. Isha waved his hand, and the Dog Soldier let go and sat down. Isha motioned for the others to stand, which they reluctantly did, refusing to maintain eye contact for more than an instant.

When Isha spoke, he did so slowly and with intention. "Each of you has been spared for a reason." Isha paused to let his words sink in and to make sure that the Arabs understood him. "Do any of you speak English?"

The Arabs were silent. Isha leaped forward at one of the men and was about to scream when the Arab stepped backward and shouted.

"Yes, yes!"

Isha paused. "All of you?"

Each man nodded his head.

"The reason will be made known to you soon. If you cooperate, I will spare your life and turn you over to the authorities. If you do not, I will kill you."

Isha's voice conveyed no emotion. His blood ran cold, and all around him could see it.

He motioned to four Dog Soldiers to grab two of the Arabs and take them outside of the cavern. Two would interrogate each Arab. They had already gone over the scenario, and knew that they had a limited time to extract the information that they needed. If the Arabs did not talk, Isha had given strict orders that they would be killed.

Isha motioned Joe to come into the room. He moved towards him. On the way, he untied Spencer. Spencer got up and moved towards Isha.

"You will interrogate these two with two of my men." Isha motioned to two of his men who were standing nearby. "I will go outside with my other men, and we will get information from the other two. We don't have much time."

Spencer could not believe what had just happened, but she simply nodded and looked at Joe. He nodded back, and Isha was on the move, headed outside.

Around the corner, Agha tightened the silencer on his Glock. He took the safety off. The group inside the cavern had moved the Arabs to the side of the big cavern room. The light was shining against that wall. Just enough darkness shrouded the opposite wall to allow Agha to move.

He began crawling cautiously against the wall on the other side of the cavern. Joe, and Spencer, along with the two Dog Soldiers, stood flanked around two of his men. They were now questioning them and providing enough noise to cover Agha's escape.

He pointed his firearm and considered killing as many as he could, but his mission was too important. Instead, he needed to escape to live another day. *El Tiburón* would supply him more men. Although Agha despised working with the drug cartel, he needed them now.

As he slid forward, Agha trained his weapon on the unsuspecting backs of his enemies. He continued to move forward and was now almost around the outside corner of the room. Agha took one last glance at his men, as he escaped around the wall. Then he rose to a crouch and walked forward slowly, looking for any sign of life. He saw none.

As he got closer to the exit of the cavern, Agha heard voices outside. He heard a slap against flesh, and the Native American leader, was yelling. He heard one of his men stammer, trying to talk.

Agha emerged from the cavern. To his left, he saw the group. The torch was lit, and his men were kneeling. The demons surrounded them, yelling at them. Agha longed to kill them, but this was not the time. He looked to his right and about one hundred yards away, by the light of a full moon, saw his SUV. He knew taking it would be a death sentence.

Up beyond the SUV, approximately a half-mile away, *El Tiburón's* men had left a "care package" for him in the event disaster struck, as it had. Ironically, *El Tiburón* had decided on a lightning fast Ducati motorcycle, which had a compartment that was packed with various supplies including a satellite phone.

Agha would make his way to the motorcycle and head south, where he would arrive at the border near Palomas, ditch the motorcycle and walk to the rendezvous point to meet *El Tiburón*.

He walked forward now, away from the scene, filing away sheer hatred for the men who had killed his brothers. He walked with a sense of purpose. These men would eventually die, including the leader. He would see to it. None of his Arabs knew the exact details of what was planned. None of them knew where and how they would unleash the terror on the Americans. It would be massive. Far more than any of them knew.

That lack of information had been Agha's design.

"Torture them all you want. None of them will talk," Agha thought. *"If they do, you will hear a story which is made up, nothing like the real terror which will soon play out."*

Agha stopped in his tracks, with panic setting in. Thirty feet ahead, a man urinated.

He crouched down and looked back, estimating the distance. He was far enough away now. And a slight wind blew.

Agha crept up, closer and closer, as the man sang something under his voice. He saw his dad again, across that field, which seemed so long ago now. Five feet away, Agha stood from his crouch, and calmly, but with determination, raised the silenced weapon and put a bullet in the back of the man's head. The Dog Soldier fell and hit the ground with a thud, dead. *The fighter plane strike had claimed another life, years later and a world away,* Agha thought. He gave him a final glance back and ran, free of the confines of the cavern, free of the captivity, and free now to unleash hell upon the Americans.

Isha looked up, thinking he had heard a strange sound. He turned to look behind him, but all he saw was darkness.

CHAPTER 18

Agha was still breathing hard as he walked away from the cave. His thoughts were on the horror that he had witnessed. The invaders didn't seem human.

Who were they?

No one had identified a Native American threat. His research had focused on the FBI and border authorities. But most of his men were now dead, and the others were captured. "*Who were these infidels that invaded the cave?*"

In all of his missions over the years, Agha had never experienced such a crushing defeat. Doubt rushed in, but he pushed it aside.

As he walked, Agha told himself over and over that he was still walking the path of destiny. These men would pay and so would thousands of Americans for the deaths of his warriors. Now he was even more determined to see to it that the weapon was unleashed. They would not stop him, no matter what.

Agha walked around a hollowed out cliff, along a trail barely visible in the moonlight. *El Tiburón* had told him to follow this trail if something went awry. He was now well out of view of the Native Americans and because of the night breeze, too far to hear them, so they could not hear him either. He deliberately paced up to the hidden cave around the backside of a bluff. He drew his firearm, keeping a lookout for any mountain lions or other animals that might be using the cave as a resting spot. As he got closer to the cave, he could see a large tree jutted out of the side of the bluff, partially obscuring the cave. The trail led him right to it.

Agha walked up to the tree and pushed aside some branches that partly covered the cave, and then he saw a shape. He stepped back, but then realized the shape was his escape: the motorcycle.

El Tiburón, in classic flair, had left him a Ducati Diavel Dark, all black, a beautifully fast bike barely visible in the darkness of the cave. On the one hand, the signature Desmodromic "roar" from its engine and the L-twin cylinder, which all Ducati enthusiasts loved, would pose a problem for a terrorist attempting to make a run for the border. That problem, however, would be offset by the sheer speed Agha would reach on the trek to Palomas, Mexico. He'd need it. He had a head start, but the roads he would take covered a distance of over two hundred fifty miles. At speeds of one hundred twenty-five miles per hour on the Ducati, he had two hours of danger before he reached the Mexican border.

Agha checked the compartment on the Ducati and found the GPS device and a map, a Sig Sauer P238 Tactical Laser pistol, with ammo, a CRKT tactical knife, a satellite phone and a water bottle.

He checked the map and GPS device and read the notes left for him. He mapped his route, and then turned on the satellite phone and sent a text message to the number he had memorized. It would go to another satellite phone, in the hands of an *El Tiburón* associate in Palomas.

"*Yo'm en mi camino.*" (I'm on my way).

Agha shut off the phone and started up the engine. In his completely dark garb, on the black Ducati, he resembled a devil bent on destruction. Only time would tell if his plan would come to fruition.

Meanwhile, twenty minutes into the interrogation of the Arabs, Isha looked around for Asija, whom he had placed on security duty when the questioning of the Arabs began.

Isha walked away from the Arabs. Asija should have been back by now to at least report. The Arabs weren't talking, and Isha had a feeling that something was wrong. He continued walking to where Asija was posted.

Inside the cave, Spencer questioned the other two Arabs with better results.

While Joe looked on, Spencer told the Arabs of their likely fate in the American criminal justice system if they did not cooperate, including a trial in a military tribunal, and likely a death sentence if they were convicted.

Spencer added: "The American authorities will hunt your family members down, and in a matter of time your bank accounts will be frozen, and everything you own seized. You have options if you cooperate. You might be able to bring your families to the United States. We already have someone within the organization in custody. We know an attack is planned. If you cooperate, you will be treated fairly."

At first the Arabs had been hard rocks, refusing to speak. Then, Joe took one of them deeper inside the cave and called on a Dog Soldier to stand guard over him. Spencer isolated the other Arab with a Dog Soldier looking on, gun drawn and at the ready. Finally, after considering his options, this one began to crack. He explained that he wanted asylum and asylum for his family. Spencer told him they could not promise anything, only that he would be treated fairly.

As they listened, the Arab traced their smuggling route through South America and into Mexico and then across the border. When Spencer asked how they had gotten across the border, he told her they had crossed in a tunnel but did not know the location.

Spencer wondered whether he was actually telling the truth about what he knew, as so far this was what she knew. The Arab described going through the checkpoint and ending up in Indian country. Spencer grilled him about some of the details, and he told her about Officer Begay, and how they got out just in time, ahead of the helicopters, from their safe house on the reservation.

Spencer shook her head, realizing they had been only minutes too late. The Arab said he hadn't been told any details of the mission, only at some point they would be given their assignments. But this had never happened. He said he overheard the leader talking on the phone about ultralight aircraft and poisoning the Americans. He said he did not know much of anything else.

Spencer listened intently and watched for clues. This relatively low-level member of the organization had just repeated to her what Bashir had also said – that the attack would be by ultralight aircraft. Such an important detail would be kept from the lower level operatives. Spencer sensed something was wrong.

"What exactly did you hear about the ultralight aircraft?"

The Arab hesitated. "I only know what I heard. The Americans would be poisoned with ultralight aircraft and some type of weapon."

Spencer saw a brief twitch and the man looked down and to the right, classic signs that he was being untruth-

155

ful. She was thinking about what to ask next when, a loud piercing cry erupted.

It was unlike any that she had heard before. It was long and guttural, like someone dying or in incredible anguish. Spencer leaped back in surprise. The Arab put his hands in the air, and a Dog Soldier pointed his weapon at him. Joe pulled his firearm. Something had just gone horribly wrong.

Outside, Isha cradled the body of the young Asija in his arms. He was dead, and way too soon. He cried out in anguish and lifted his gaze to the heavens.

Thunder Hawk and another Dog Soldier reached him and saw him holding their fallen brother. They stopped within five yards of Isha, understanding the need to give him this moment by himself. Unable to contain himself any longer, Isha sobbed, at first quietly and then loudly, as he pulled Asija tighter and tighter to his grieving body.

Agha was passing Quemado, New Mexico. He stopped to take a drink of water. The Ducati was running smoothly. It had been an uneventful ride so far, and he had heard and seen next to nothing, which was for the best. He checked his watch. It was 4:00 a.m.

He had a few hours before sunlight and had to get to Palomas before then. When he hit Silver City it would be only about an hour farther, and then he'd be home free. He revved the engine and sped off again into the night.

When Isha arose holding the young Dog Soldier's body,
he turned around to face Thunder Hawk and his fellow Dog Soldiers.

They backed up when they saw Isha's eyes, which were as cold as stone, seemingly drained of life. Yet they also betrayed a deadly undercurrent inside Isha, a Gorgon stare that was frightening and mesmerizing.

Isha motioned and Thunder Hawk took Asija's body, gently cradling him. The other Dog Soldiers joined in, and they carried Asija's body as Isha walked in front.

When they got back to the cavern, Isha summoned everyone to a meeting outside. Joe, Spencer and the Dog Soldiers emerged from the cave. The Dog Soldiers lined the Arabs up next to each other, sitting on the ground. As Isha paced in front of them, they started to shudder involuntarily. Spencer began to say something, but Joe placed his arm on hers, and she stopped herself from speaking.

When Isha spoke, it was in almost a whisper. "The time for talk is over. I have but one question. Who escaped?"

Isha stared hard at the Arabs.

"Look up at me!" His voice boomed.

The first Arab looked up and trembled uncontrollably. He watched in stunned horror as Isha morphed in and out of his spirit animal.

Isha pulled his knife and started towards the first Arab. When he did so, the third Arab, the first Arab's brother, spoke up.

"No. No more violence! The man who escaped is Agha! He is the leader. He is heading for the border of Mexico."

"Where in Mexico?"

"He will go to Juarez to meet with the drug dealer. They are to meet and unleash the weapon."

With those words, Spencer bolted and ran to an available vehicle. She dialed an emergency number to SAC Bowman. She related what had happened, including her kidnapping at the motel. Then she hurriedly told him the rest of the events, including the apparent escape of the leader, Agha.

She demanded that FBI and state police be sent to their location to retrieve the Arabs, related the debrief comments of the Arab about the ultralights, and the comment that the other Arab had made just now that Agha was headed towards Juarez.

Spencer now knew that the ultralight story was a ruse, and that the real story had just come out: Agha and *El Tiburón* would find a way to unleash the weapon, likely in El Paso, by simply crossing the border with it.

SAC Bowman was now wide awake: "Stay put Spencer. We need to guard the Arabs, and I will send backup ASAP. You are not to head to the border under any circumstances. Is that clear?"

Spencer said she understood and hung up.

As she turned and approached Isha and the others, she could see that Isha had given orders. Joe was moving, and Spencer went over to him.

"Where are you going?"

"Agent, the others will stay here and wait with the Arabs. I am going to track Agha's whereabouts to the border, and I will call you."

"I am going with you," Spencer insisted, not remotely planning to stay put.

Joe looked at her and nodded his head. He knew it was futile to try and resist at this point.

"Agent, we may need the FBI's assistance once we find him. So you are free to come, but when it comes to tracking Agha, stay the hell out of my way."

Joe did not leave any room for argument in his comment, and Spencer nodded her head.

Isha joined them as they walked towards the spot where Asija had been killed. Joe saw the blood and identified Asija's footprints. He shined his flashlight and spied Agha's prints. They made a definite impression in the soil.

"Here! This is him, Joe."

Spencer was pointing at the ground.

Joe nodded. He put his hand on Isha's shoulder.

"We will find him Isha. That I promise."

"Find him but don't kill him. I will bury Asija. And then I will come and find you all."

Isha turned and he was gone.

CHAPTER 19

Joe and Spencer traced the footprints. He was having a lot of trouble dealing with his thoughts, and what he had just seen. It was shocking in the extreme.

Not since combat had he witnessed death and destruction like that.

That was violent. And Isha didn't hesitate.

He took a moment to step behind his vehicle and drink from a small bottle. The intoxicating liquid calmed him a bit, but he couldn't shake the sense of panic that he felt from the sheer deadliness of the cave.

Darkness surrounded them now. Even though he was having difficulty focusing, he had a mission to accomplish. Joe shook his head and turned his thoughts back to the task at hand.

The darkness made it more difficult as they had to locate individual prints and could not look forward. Joe knew that Agha had taken some type of vehicle if he was going to make it to the border.

As they continued to walk, Spencer received a phone call.

"Hello, this is Bowman. We have Agents on their way. The Arabs are to remain stationary and in lockdown custody, is that understood?"

"Yes, sir."

"Maria, we have obtained presidential approval and launched a couple of Predator drones from Fort Huachuca. They are preparing to leave now. I need to know what to tell the operators about the vehicle that Agha is operating. We intend to find him before harm is done. I can't stress enough that this is now the highest priority mission in the United States. A BOLO (be on the lookout) notice has been sent to every law enforcement agency on this side of the border. We must find this guy! There's just one more thing, SSA Spencer, good work."

She could not help but smile faintly.

"Ok, I understand. We are trying to gather that information, and we will get back to you ASAP."

She hung up and realized that Joe was now thirty or so yards ahead of her, and his flashlight was growing dimmer as he moved away. She jogged to catch up.

Spencer was excited. "Joe, we need to figure out what kind of vehicle Agha is in, if that's possible. We are actively looking for him."

Joe shook his head and nodded, but the thought crossed his mind: *What the hell do you think I'm doing here, Agent?*

Joe refused to look up from the ground and the signs he was seeing. The faint prints, broken branches and impressions in the ground, took them around a bluff. Now, they walked on more rocky terrain. Joe could see only the faintest disturbance of soil and small rocks continued to lead him in the same direction. He shined his flashlight forward.

Ahead, about fifteen yards, Joe spotted a tree. It appeared to have branches that had been pulled back. Joe motioned to Spencer and slowly walked towards them. When he got within five yards, Joe saw that the tree partially obscured what looked to be a cavern behind it. One of the tree branches hung at an angle, having been broken. It was recent. He turned to Spencer who nodded.

As they passed by the tree and walked inside the cave, Joe saw signature tire track marks and disturbed dirt on the floor of the cave. There were two tires, not four.

Agha is on a motorcycle.

While Joe wasn't intimately familiar with motorcycle tires, he took photographs of the imprint and emailed them from his phone to a friend of his who was. Joe's friend messaged him back inside a minute, as Jose continued to look around the cave for clues.

Hey, dip-shit, thanks for the early morning wake up call. Those are Pirelli tires. Racing bike, may be a Ducati.

Joe showed the text to Spencer and then looked around a little longer but didn't see anything of interest.

Spencer radioed the message to Bowman that Agha was on a motorcycle, possibly a Ducati.

Seconds later, that message was relayed to the military command center, which relayed the information to the Predator operators.

U.S. Customs and Border Protection Agencies operate four Predator MQ-9s out of Fort Huachuca. The MQ-9s are equipped with GA-ASI's Lynx synthetic aperture radar and Raytheon's MTS-B electro-optical infrared sensors.

They can "see" images at night just as well as they can be seen in the day. The Predator can spot the heat signature of an individual human being at an altitude of twenty-thousand feet. Both are also equipped with the ARGUS-IS system.

For this mission, they were also equipped with two Hellfire missiles each. Although authorization to fire had not been given, the President reserved the right to do so if necessary.

The distance from Sierra Vista, Arizona, where Fort Huachuca was housed, to Deming, New Mexico, was just over two hundred miles. The MQ-9s could be over the Deming sky in about forty-five minutes, from the moment that the operators got the message.

They were already firing up, with one mission ahead: to find the most dangerous Arab in the United States at the moment, on a motorcycle, bound for the Mexican border. Once found, every agent in the vicinity would be alerted to descend on him with one order: Shoot to kill.

Just as the MQ-9s were lifting off from Fort Huachuca, Agha was arriving in Deming, New Mexico. He stopped briefly just past Deming on the side of the road to send one more text message, which was promptly received by an *El Tiburón* associate in Palomas:

Inicie los ultraligeros en bente minutos.
(Launch the ultralights in twenty minutes.)

Agha revved the engine and sped back onto the road towards Columbus, New Mexico. After Columbus, he would cross the border and be in Palomas, Mexico. It would take him less than thirty minutes more to make it to the international border and into Mexico.

Joe and Spencer were en route to El Paso, Texas at a high rate of speed. She talked excitedly about what they had learned and what would soon happen. It seemed to her that Agha could not escape. They had him. They would get to the border, relay information to the military and the Predators would take over. They would stop this attack.

El Tiburón and ten of his most trusted guards waited for them just across the international border. They were guarding two air tight sealed containers, of the deadly Ebola-pox virus.

El Tiburón had not told his CIA handlers about the canisters. It had been part of his plan all along.

While he would help them trace drugs that the cartel was running, guns from other cartels, but he wouldn't tell them about the containers. That was something he had chosen to keep secret.

In the end, *El Tiburón* was loyal only to himself. He had his own motives for wanting the Arabs' plan to work: the price for smuggling would increase ten-fold after an attack like this, and so would the CIA's payments for his information. It would mean that *El Tiburón* would prosper even more.

Also waiting in a farm just past Ascension, Mexico, were two ultralight aircraft that were ready at a moment's notice to take off towards the American border and Columbus, New Mexico. The pilots would soon become martyrs.

CHAPTER 20

As Agha neared Columbus, New Mexico, he throttled down on the Ducati. He looked ahead at the dim lights stretched out across that sleepy border city. The sun had not risen above the horizon.

Agha was getting desperate to get through the border and to Janos, Mexico. He needed to contact *El Tiburón*.

He slowed slightly. He began to think about how much longer it would take him to cross. So far, Allah had smiled upon him. Agha was fewer than ten miles from the border of Mexico and once he crossed, he would start the final stages of the terror plan.

The vision of his father crossing that fateful field flashed across his head. Then, the explosion, and his father was no more. The violence had been too much. Now he would return it.

Agha breathed the calm night air, and whispered to himself, *I will not fail now. It is my destiny. I am in the land of my enemy, and they can't stop me. All of their technology, their supposed superior forces, and I am able to ride through their country, unseen on a motorcycle. I will kill as many as I can.*

He felt a surge of adrenaline go through his body. He also felt a renewed confidence, bordering on arrogance, at his ability to slip past the American authorities over and over again.

As he breezed past the first several houses on the outskirts of town, he saw nothing unusual, other than a few rabbits jumping across the street ahead of him.

To the east, he noticed the first streaks of daylight emerging from behind the mountains. He knew that he had to make the border before the sun came up.

Agha cleared the first intersection in town. He looked in each direction, everything looked clear until he saw them. Police cars positioned one hundred yards to the right on a side street. His heart was almost beating out of his chest and his adrenaline was pumping. He quickly realized that there were at least ten patrol cars with their lights off. They were outside the vehicles talking.

Agha slowed to try to pass them without getting their attention. As he pulled in adjacent to them, his lights gave him away.

"Stop!" "That's him!" A policeman yelled. "That's him! That's him!"

Agha turned to the voice and saw the police were running. People were barking orders. He then heard car doors opening, and slamming shut.

This is do or die. They are coming to get me.

Agha lowered his head and punched it. The Ducati screamed to life and accelerated to breakneck speed that would have made its Italian crafters proud. The front wheel rose off the ground as he bore down hard on his target, the Mexican border.

Cop cars to the right were roaring and screeching their tires, peeling out, heading towards the main roadway to try and stop him.

Agha was fast approaching the port of entry between Columbus, New Mexico and Palomas, Mexico. Two canopies rose over the entrances and exits. One points southbound into Mexico and one opens northbound into the United States. An adjacent guard station is designed so that authorities can check the southbound vehicles as they enter the canopy. The whole idea is that the southbound vehicles will stop and wait for the guard to check them and wave them through.

Agha had other intentions. At this point his Ducati was flying at almost one hundred-sixty miles per hour.

The sides of the roadway were screaming by so fast that Agha could not tell what he was passing. Had an animal crossed the roadway at that moment, Agha would have been dead. He leaned down further into the Ducati. He was going through the port of entry no matter what. He looked, with the backdrop of the now rising sun, and morning light, like a dark ghost horse, blazing ahead at breakneck speed, incapable of being stopped by any human force.

As the Mexican guard emerged from his station and ran into the opening of the canopy headed southbound, he shouted. "*¡Para!*" (Stop!)

One hand was raised, while holding his gun in the other. His expression changed from authoritarian to sheer terror in an instant, as he saw the gigantic black bullet flying towards him like lightning, about to cut him in half.

The guard had just enough time to dive right. As he did, he felt Agha and his Ducati whiz by, cutting a hole through the space where the guard had just been standing.

The guard hit the dirt hard and his handgun bounced forward a few feet from him. He raised his head and looked back. The motorcycle was flying. He heard a barrage of shots ring out from the American side. He ducked his head into the dirt.

The Americans launched what seemed like an arsenal. The fusillade of rounds kept going forever it seemed. The guard had seen port runners before, but never with this intense a reaction. His head down, the guard could still hear the whine of the engine. The shots died down as the mysterious rider fled on, in the direction of Janos, Mexico, to the south.

The MQ-9 predators reached the area between Deming and Columbus in somewhat record speed. Because it was classified, their true speed had not been released to the public. The actual speed was remarkably faster than anyone knew. With the ARGUS system cameras perched on the bottom of the predators, their operators arrived in the area in time to see the crazed scene that was playing out beneath the predators, thousands of feet below.

The man on the motorcycle cut a heat signature that seemed to streak across the earth, way ahead of the myriad of cop cars that followed behind. He rocketed through the port of entry and into Mexico as one of the predators locked him and had him tracked on its computer screen. It would be as easy as the push of a button to launch the Hellfire missiles. They readied to fire and turn him into a plume of smoke.

Although he was now in Mexico, the President of the United States and the President of Mexico had decided that this man was a live target and a national security threat. He could and would be shot down by either authority on sight, even if the border issues were somewhat sketchy. Those would be dealt with at a later time. The main issue was taking this man out.

To this end, Mexican authorities had launched several UH-60 Blackhawk Helicopters from Chihuahua, Mexico. They were now heading towards the kill zone air space, also close enough to launch an attack against the fugitive terrorist.

But sometimes it is better to be lucky than good. At the moment when the American authorities were about to make their decision to launch Hellfire missiles from the predators, and very shortly before the Mexican authorities would make their similar decision of how to use their helicopters, ARGUS cameras picked up the flight pattern of two ultralight aircraft that had taken off somewhere near Ascension, Mexico.

Alarm bells went off. The operators of the predators immediately signaled their military superiors, and the calls went up the chain to the desk of the president within minutes. Support staff had enabled a command and control screen for the president to review. He and his advisors were now looking at the rapid approach of ultralight aircraft towards the United States border near Columbus, New Mexico.

The debrief of Bashir and some of the other Arabs in *El Malpais* had yielded consistent details: an attack was coming by ultralight aircraft, and it would be extreme and would involve a catastrophic biological weapon.

One of the lone detractors had been Special Agent Maria Spencer. She believed that the ultralight attack was a ruse, and she expected an attack on foot with terrorists carrying the weapon near El Paso, Texas or some other border area. But Bowman had dismissed her, as had others.

Now, it looked like Bowman had been right. The president did not hesitate. The order to shoot down the ultralights was given, and was relayed to the operators of the predators.

The tracking box on the predator screen was removed from Agha seconds before the Hellfire missile would have been launched. Instead, they changed direction and locked in on the incoming ultralight craft. It took less than ten seconds, and the missiles were fired.

Agha looked up as he raced ahead, and blinding light streaked across the sky. Then, to the north of him, two massive explosions rocked the earth, resounding loudly for miles. The sky was lit as bright as day. Plumes of smoke and pieces of aircraft fell to the earth. Agha slowed and watched as the remnants of what must have been the ultralights breathed its last and fell to its death. The plan had worked. Agha smiled and raced ahead to Janos.

Above the scene the hunter-killer MQ-9 predators turned and altered course to head back to Fort Huachuca. Their mission was accomplished.

The higher ups shouted and smiled enthusiastically as they watched what they believed to be the end of the worst terror threat to the United States in over a decade.

In Washington, D.C., the President saw the destruction on a series of screens. He turned to his advisors and they all nodded in unison. The terrorist threat had indeed been eliminated, without loss of human life, in a remote area, away from human population, near the border. The President was already going through in his mind elements of the speech that he would prepare for delivery to the general public. He allowed himself a small smile as he realized, his next term of office was almost a lock.

The President picked up his phone and dialed another advisor. He ordered that the CDC units that had been stationed nearby in case of an attack were to descend on the scene immediately.

The ultralights' wreckage lay just shy of the United States border, and the Mexican Blackhawks were still en route. The CDC personnel were to coordinate with Mexican authorities and report back whether there was any need for quarantine, and what steps needed to be taken next.

The incoming flash reports from the ARGUS computers would not be sufficient to determine whether any chemical had been leaked or whether chemical remained intact in the downed crafts.

The president of Mexico had pre-authorized elite military units from the United States to respond to the scene and coordinate with Mexican military to survey the scene where the aircraft pieces had fallen to obtain any evidence from the shrapnel, and to secure it.

The President allowed himself to sit down when this was done, and grabbed a Scotch that his Chief of Staff had just placed in front of him.

The mood in the situation room had turned from tension to extreme relief. He grabbed the glass, glanced at his chief, smiled and took a sip.

The Scotch, Johnny Walker Blue, tasted very sweet at this moment. The worry and stress were already beginning to fade away. The public had no idea the amount of responsibility that he carried on his shoulders. It was almost inconceivable. Today, things had gone right.

The chief raised his thumb to him in victory. Soon every TV and news outlet across the country would report the president's speech, including that a monumental terror attack had been put down by the governments of the United States and Mexico in a joint effort, with intelligence provided by the FBI. This was almost too good to be true. Yes, indeed, this was going to be a good night.

In all of the celebratory aftermath, the authorities decided to let Agha go, in the short window that they had to stop him. The real threat had always been the ultra-lights. They would send in a team to get Agha later. There was always time, now it's time to celebrate.

Relieved, Agha stopped the Ducati in Janos, Mexico, safe at last. He made a few final turns and pulled up to the house where *El Tiburón* waited. The door opened.

Out stepped *El Tiburón* in his signature black cowboy hat. He had a semi-automatic machine gun strapped over his shoulder.

"*Hola*, what took you so long, Agha? Good to see you my friend."

El Tiburón laughed. He and Agha embraced.

"Almost did not make it. We need to get inside."

El Tiburón waved Agha into the house and patted him on the back. As they walked inside, *El Tiburón's* men took the cycle behind the house and placed it inside a garage, away from the eyes of any surveillance.

"*El Tiburón*, it is good to see you. You are aware now that I am the only one left. We must still deliver the weapon. You have it here, no?"

Agha sat down at a wooden table across from El Tiburón. He nodded and snapped his fingers. A woman ran into the room with two shots of tequila.

El Tiburón grabbed his shot and took a long sip. He held his glass up to Agha, who did the same. Agha, in contravention of laws of Islam, took a sip of the alcohol, smaller than *El Tiburón's*. To say the least, it had been a very stressful few days.

"My fee must include an additional two million United States dollars. We had to get through a blockade, thanks to you, to get over to Janos, on Highway 2 from Juarez. We carried this through the blockade."

El Tiburón now stretched out his hands to show the two metal containers, which held the canisters of deadly virus. Agha almost fell as he tried to stand up and stepped backwards.

He put his hands up and said, "Ok, yes, it's ok."

El Tiburón involuntarily laughed. He gently handed the container back to his guard who placed it inside another airtight container.

"*El Tiburón* , we must change our plans. We will launch something else first. To create a diversion. El Paso is dangerous right now."

"We can still bring the containers in through the border into El Paso," *El Tiburón* replied.

"We can take three vehicles. You, me, and ten of my most trusted guards who are waiting for my call. When we get to the border, guides will bring us across and into the city. My men and I will leave once we are safe at the border, and you have met up with the guides. Now, I will wait for you to make the call to transfer the money."

Agha dialed on his satellite phone.

In a remote clearing, on the side of a bluff near Window Rock, Arizona, Isha and his Dog Soldiers sat in a circle, meditating and chanting softly.

A fire pit lit up the circle's center. Isha was replaying all of the scenes of the cave in his mind, focusing his concentration on the man, the leader, who had killed Asija and gotten away. They gave him a traditional burial.

Now Isha thought about the leader, the same man whom he had seen at the motel in Gallup.

As he breathed and meditated, taking it all in, Isha saw the man, saw that he was still alive. Felt his evil presence. He lit a cigarette made from Peyote.

He passed it first to Thunder Hawk and then around the circle of men. They all took it in and their minds began to clear. Time stopped. They were preparing to travel now.

As the drug made its way through their synapses, and into their souls, lightness took over their being.

Isha opened his eyes. "We go. It is time to end this."

CHAPTER 21

After explaining how he escaped the cave, Agha excused himself from *El Tiburón* and stepped outside the safe house onto a covered porch in the rear.

He looked right and left and upwards, careful to not expose himself to the searching eyes of whatever aircraft was hunting for him. He pulled out a satellite "burner" phone. He looked into the desert and dialed.

The first call was to the leader of the eight men who had headed north into Colorado. He reached them at their safe house on the outskirts of Denver, where they'd been hiding since Gallup.

They informed Agha that they had sent coded messages to several "sleeper cells." The group linked up with two jihadists who had been living in Denver for six years. They worked jobs in grocery stores during this time, and patiently waited to be notified.

These and other "cells" across the country waited for the signal at which time they would be awakened. It was then, the elders told them, when they would unleash terror inside the United States, at a coordinated day and time for "Judgment Day." That day was fast approaching.

The leader told Agha they were motivated and ready to act upon his orders.

He smiled and thought, *"They had not all been killed. War was like that; one had to adapt."*

Half of his group was still in place, and he was alive and out of the lion's den. The operation would go on.

Agha told the leader to wait for now, and he would get back to them soon.

His next call was to a jack-of-all-trades to the cartel. He was an amateur mechanic in Mexico before the cartel made him a more lucrative offer.

Bashir's organization had paid for ten ultralight aircraft. For Agha, the mechanic equipped the ultralight aircraft with compact but very powerful firebombs. It had taken a long time to modify the aircraft by adding fuel tanks to increase their range.

The ultralights were destined to fly into the interior of the United States to various locations. A potent firebomb assembled with a large volume of flammable liquid, an ignitor, and bomb components to spread the liquid, were attached to the bottom of all ten ultralight crafts. The pilots would parachute to safety shortly before the intended crash destination, and altimeter devices would detonate the bombs at one hundred feet or so before impact, spreading the flames in a wide radius.

The ultralights were sitting in a large warehouse near Denver. From Denver, the jihadists would launch them to set wild fires in Colorado, Arizona, Nevada, New Mexico, Wyoming and Montana.

Agha was about to tell the mechanic to give the signal to the jihadists. When that signal was given, the mechanic would contact another man.

That man would access the deep web and post the most ominous message that the United States had ever seen: in Arabic, it said simply:

Operation Judgment Day is here.

That message would launch the terror plot. The jihadists, who had been holed up near Denver, would leave in the dead of night, headed to their particular destinations to set the fires.

Agha's plan was that one Jihadist would go to each state where they'd planned to set fires, except in Colorado, where a monumental fire had been planned and required the service of four men. The Arab pilots would find their respective ultralight crafts and fly them into the desired areas. The pilots would bail out before the ultralights crashed into the earth, and shortly before the firebombs detonated and sent highly flammable liquids and flame into a wide area around the crash. The goal was simple: set large, hot, engulfing wild fires simultaneously across the Western United States.

Agha spent a good deal of time selecting the places and locations where the fires would be set. No one had known the full scope of the plan except him. The initial two ultralights had been a ruse, and the Americans had bit.

Authorities had long speculated that Al Qaeda was involved with setting wild fires on United States soil. No law enforcement agency had yet made a definitive arrest on that basis, but the media was awash in stories that claimed a terror link. The figures on the destruction and monetary loss of wild fires were staggering.

In any given year, over a billion dollars in property damage and insurance claims could be attributed to raging Western wild fires. This did not account for the cost of human lives lost. Recently, and tragically, numerous "hot shot" fire fighters had died in response to fires in Arizona.

This was real terror and the public was slow to get it. The part about setting fires, Agha always thought, was that it was nearly impossible to catch the persons responsible.

He had long believed that subtle forms of terror were the best idea. Grandiose plans and one-shot acts might make a splash in the media, but to really win the battle against the Americans, one had to have a long-term approach. In this game of terror, a little was a lot, especially with an already battered economy, hitting the Americans repeatedly on multiple fronts, including setting widespread wild fires, would weaken them to the point that they might break. Likely it would come from within.

The Americans had a long tradition of rising up against tyranny and oppression.

Agha knew that given time, and a weakening and unstable economy, tempers would rise, armed men would take matters into their own hands, and a revolution would foment and boil over. In the midst of that revolution, America would be weak and easily exploited by outside forces.

In his imagination, Agha could visualize it all, but first, they needed to set the fires. He gave the signal.

The time is now.

The man in Rocky Point made the call. The other man fired up the internet and sent the message:

Operation Judgment Day has begun.

In less than thirty minutes, the sleeper cells had awakened. Jihadists across the United States packed their bags and necessary supplies. Bashir's laundering organization had arranged for transportation for them to Denver, and then the location where they would launch.

Later, in the early morning darkness of the following day, the jihadists launched all ten ultralight aircraft simultaneously.

They flew off bound for their destination points with their cargo: highly flammable, incendiary bombs.

Agha hoped a majority of them would be successful. If they were, massive fires would soon burn hot across the western United States. It would take weeks, even months to contain.

The cost of fighting all of these fires at the same time would be enormous, as he had hoped. More importantly, the fires would occupy the authorities.

Agha went back inside the safe house and took a seat on a tattered couch across from *El Tiburón* and three of his men.

He was smoking a cigar, puffing and blowing rings of smoke into the air above them all.

On the coffee table between them were several beers and a bottle of Tequila. Agha leaned forward and grabbed a bottle of beer. He looked at it and popped the top off. Agha took a long pull at the beer as *El Tiburón* and the others looked on.

"How was it in the cave? How did it feel knowing that your men were being killed?"

He was testing Agha. He grabbed a shot from the bottle of tequila and downed it quickly. Then he poured another.

Agha paused and shook his head back and forth a few times. He didn't say anything for a moment. He then looked up and caught *El Tiburón's* eyes.

"I watched some demons take the lives of my men, my comrades, my friends. They were savages. I could not stop it. It made me sick, but more determined."

El Tiburón paused and paid attention. He leaned forward a bit in his seat.

"So I vowed to escape. To cause them harm when I could, and it happened almost as soon as I left the cave. One of their guards, one of these Natives, he was watching for us, a guard, as they questioned my men who were still alive. I got close enough to see him, and then I raised my gun and I shot him in the back of the head. He fell but he wasn't dead from the shot right away. I walked up, and I watched him. His leg was turned under him. His arms were out at the sides, and his face was in the dirt. Blood was gushing out of his head. Do you understand *El Tiburón*? I caused that, the rush of the blood. He was trying to breathe. I leaned down and put some of the blood on my fingers. And smelled it. The life running out of him."

He paused.

"I whispered to him that he would die because he dared to oppose my *Jihad*. I watched him breathe a few more times and die. His blood for the blood of my men who were killed in the cave. I grabbed his head after he died and raised it a bit and looked into his eyes. He looked strong. Like a true warrior. I killed him and now I will get their leader. It is just a matter of time. They ambushed us, but they are weak. I will kill them all before it is over, *El Tiburón*."

There was nothing in Agha's eyes as he spoke. No emotion, just darkness.

El Tiburón was nodding his head, but even he was caught off guard by the calm, cool demeanor and complete lack of emotion. He sipped a beer as he listened to the account from Agha.

"I found the motorcycle. Thank you for leaving it for me. I outran the police and made it through the checkpoint. Do you know what I thought during the whole ride? I killed their sentry, it was then I knew, they are vulnerable just like the rest of the Americans."

El Tiburón continued to eye Agha. He nodded again. He took a few more pulls on his beer. He had been at this a long time and knew killers when he saw them. Agha was definitely one of the killers. There was coldness, professionalism, and hardness in his eyes.

"Agha, these things happen. I am glad you are here and ok. What is our next step?"

"The next step is already in motion."

"You mean the Africans? My men are bringing them now. They are wearing masks, are they sick?" He paused. "No matter, it's not my business."

Just then the door opened and Agha saw his final two men, both from Guinea, West Africa. The cartel smuggled them to Brazil and then drove them up to the Mexican border. Both had been exposed to the Ebola virus about ten days before. One of them coughed repeatedly into his mask. Agha signaled and they were out the door, *El Tiburón* in the lead.

The ultralights and their pilots were now inbound to their crash destinations. In New Mexico, the ultralight pilot attempted to parachute just before he crashed in

Los Alamos Canyon. He had planned to crash as close as possible to the Los Alamos National Laboratory, and its facilities. However, the pilot was unable to free himself and went down with the ship, crashing head first into the canyon.

In Colorado, the pilot was more successful, and was able to eject just before his craft crashed into Missionary Ridge in Durango, Colorado. This site was chosen because it was the site of a massive fire in 2002, with over forty million in associated losses and firefighting costs. The ridge was again set ablaze when the ultralight crashed into it.

The pilot died, however, suspended in a tree, after his parachute lines got tangled in the tree and wrapped around his neck.

One by one, the other ultralights ended their flights and crashed head first into remote, forested areas in Nevada, Arizona and Wyoming.

When they hit the earth, metal shards flew and the firebombs exploded, throwing highly flammable liquid all over the surrounding terrain.

The burning flames expanded from the crash site very quickly because of the weather conditions. Soon, massive fires were raging. Each of those pilots chose not to parachute and became martyrs.

The planned Montana fire failed to catch. Strangely, the ultralight bound for a Montana mountain peak hit a power line on the way and blew it and its pilot into a thousand pieces. The pilot had been unable to see much right before the accident. No lights could be seen anywhere near.

The last four flew their ultralights north from Denver past Boulder and towards the town of Estes Park, near the Rocky Mountain National Park area.

The Rocky Mountain National Park is located northwest of Boulder, Colorado. Roosevelt, Routt and Arapahoe National Forests surround it. The Continental Divide runs through it as do the headwaters of the Colorado River.

The Park has beautiful mountain views and lakes. Elk, mule deer, mountain lions, moose and bears roamed through the beautiful landscape.

It was peaceful at the moment right before the Arabs emerged from the sky.

The jihadists' plan was to parachute into a designated area on Trial Ridge Road to avoid detection by ground radar systems. The road connects the town of Estes Park to Grand Lake in the west. The road reaches an elevation of 12,183 feet, with long stretches above the tree line. It crossed the Continental Divide at Milner Pass. At this time of year, in late June, it was warm, with occasional afternoon thunderstorms. This had been a very dry summer. Agha had planned it all out.

As with many plans, though, this one did not go as drawn up. One of the jihadist pilots decided to bail early, and was picked up on radar as he parachuted out too high. A search and rescue plane was launched from a nearby city, on the idea that a small plane may have gone down. As the pilots parachuted over a spot near Estes Park, the search and rescue plane was inbound.

The Arab pilots watched as their four ultralights screamed downward and smashed, without warning, into the midst of a large herd of elk. Just before the ultralights hit the ground, the firebombs ignited and flames exploded violently, outward and over a very broad area. The elk jumped and scattered at the explosions, but for some of them it was too late. Flames engulfed two of the fleeing beasts; they fell and struggled for a bit, but the fire was too much, and the animals succumbed.

The flames lit up the wilderness like the sun. They spread rapidly throughout the dry wilderness and forest are as small timber burned, and then the fire consumed larger plants and trees until it became a raging force that was too big to die by itself and capable of endless consumption. Animals died by the droves. Whole swaths of land were engulfed. Blackness spread everywhere.

Interagency Hotshot Crews (IHCs) were dispatched to the various fires through coordination out of the National Interagency Fire Center in Boise, Idaho. Hotshot crews typically involve twenty firefighters who undergo intensive, specialized training in wildfire suppression tactics.

The hotshots are elite firefighters and would need all their skill to fight the ultralight fires.

Within an hour, as authorities were scrambling to respond to the fires in the various states, the fire west of Estes Park continued to ignite and grow outward with terrifying speed. Because of weather and climate conditions in the area where that particular ultralight crashed, the fire grew into a raging inferno.

Part of the response team included ten Cheyenne Indians. One of them happened to be a Dog Soldier, and a friend of Isha's.

Hotshots know that sometimes the unpredictability of wind and terrain conditions can cause a fire to change course and direction on a dime. On this day, the Colorado fire did just that. The wind abruptly changed directions, so did the fire. The hotshots sent out a warning signal through their ranks.

As they surveyed the available escape routes, the best route seemed to be down a canyon and across a stream, which would be a natural fire-break. The only problem with the route would be that once they dipped into the canyon, they would lose eyes on the fire, and not know how quickly the raging inferno leaped forward after them.

The leader of the team made the decision. They would move out and move out quickly, head into and out of the canyon, and cross the stream to safety. But the fire was too fast, too massive. As they entered the canyon and lost sight of the fire, they also faced a terrain situation they had not seen earlier. Very tough brush was growing throughout the canyon, and slowed their movement considerably. The hotshots' nerves began to kick in. The leader ordered them to begin cutting a path and to move, move.

Before they could exit the canyon to safety, the fire surrounded the canyon walls all around, creating a ring around the canyon, and the hotshots. The smoke began to swirl and sink into the canyon itself.

The hotshots knew the situation was now desperate, but no one lost his cool and ran.

The elite firefighters each took out and deployed their fire shelters. The fire shelters were designed to withstand very high heat and protect the firefighters as the fire whooshed over their heads. The plan was to shield themselves until the fire could move on and over them and away, allowing them then to escape.

As the fire, like a monster, began its move into the canyon itself, the hotshots sat quietly inside their fire shelters, waiting for the hell to pass. The flames licked forward, and timber crackled and popped. The heat grew closer and closer. The leader spoke into his radio. He told his men to remain in their shelters and to stay calm.

The fire shelters were not built to withstand direct flames, but did provide protection and oxygen from the hot winds and poisonous gases. Those members of the team who had survived fires before by using their fire shelters knew how hellish the experience was. One of them had described it to a team member as getting run over by a freight train. The hotshots hunkered down, wrapped in their shelters.

But the air proved to be too hot. The superheated air is what firefighters fear the most, and ultimately what is deadly. The white hot air in this canyon, on this fateful day, burned and seared the lung tissue of these brave heroes, the Montana hotshots, as the fire roared over them.

The hotshot team, which included the Cheyenne and Dog Soldier, succumbed to the air and lost their lives.

In Arizona and New Mexico, the fires did not kill those who had devoted themselves to stopping them, but they did consume homes and the precious possessions of their owners.

The Los Alamos fire, before it was contained, almost destroyed important components of the national lab facilities.

The property destruction from all of the raging fires nationwide would prove to be immense. The fires had already taken innocent lives, destroyed homes, and wiped out an enormous number of wildlife, and it was just the beginning.

The President, his team, and the Department of Justice officials were reeling. CDC and Mexican officials did extensive testing around the ultralight crash sites, where the predators shot them down. They did not detect any chemical or biological weapons. Further inspection had revealed that there wasn't anything deadly at all about those ultralights.

The Attorney General and his staff grilled FBI officials from the top down to SAC Bowman about the source of information and what had gone wrong. It was apparent now to everyone that a coordinated attacks probably a terror attack had been launched, just not the way they had counted on. It would have made Sun Tzu proud.

America had been duped and right now it was a given that the country was not going to recover any time soon.

CHAPTER 22

A Dog Soldier in Montana called Isha and told him about the fires.

Shortly after, the Council of Forty-four recalled Isha and his team to Colorado. Terrorists had attacked. Isha and his team were to find the responsible parties.

He clenched the phone in his hand. His temples burned with heat. He told his men to pack up. They were headed north.

Thunder Hawk asked Joe and Spencer to come: "We need you to come to Colorado. We must find and track the people responsible for the fires. We need your help now."

Joe looked at Spencer. They had reached Las Cruces, New Mexico, but now it was time to turn north. Spencer shook her head in anger and thought of every curse word imaginable. She said half of them as her temper flared. Bashir had lied. The ultralight "attack" was something altogether different. Power grids? Wildfires?

"Of course Daniel. We will come." Spencer replied.

They knew the final battle would occur there in Colorado. They had no choice but to go.

At a seminar years ago, a specialist had briefed Spencer and others about growing intelligence that Al Qaeda may try to light fires with "ember bombs." A group of researchers, though, had largely discredited these ideas in a study done in California. They concluded

188

that the ember bombs weren't capable of causing such a raging fire.

Based on these findings, everyone, including the Bureau, had just gone back to studying other methods of potential vulnerability.

Now Spencer realized that they had been wrong. The terrorists were capable of setting large, massive fires and greatly harming the United States.

She burned hot at Bashir. He had blatantly misled her and would pay for that. No doubt SAC Bowman would be furious. Spencer's career was, pretty much over, so she had nothing to lose at this point.

"Let's go, Joe. Isha needs us, I'm there! Get us to the El Paso Airport! I will get us flights to Denver."

Joe was already on it and speeding towards the international airport in El Paso.

As they locked eyes, Joe placed his hand on Spencer's shoulder. The look of shock in her eyes was something Joe had seen before, in combat, and in the Arizona Mountains, with the famed Shadow Wolves, during a particularly rough operation. She looked up, and then put her head down and leaned into Joe, and the tears began to fall.

Isha and his team were traveling through ancient pathways to Estes Park, Colorado. They would be there soon. They felt as though the peyote was carrying them to their destination. Isha had no more tears. Instead, he felt intense emotion and determination. He vowed, after this was done, that he would find the Arabs.

One other group of people was also bound for Colorado. Agha, Begay, and the two West Africans had made it across the border. They were now on a private jet,

189

arranged and paid for by Bashir, headed to Denver, with the sealed containers in hand. Agha was going to finish this. And no one, not even the Native demons, would stop him now.

CHAPTER 23

Headquarters sent the pilot of the search and rescue helicopter real time information over his headset, but he didn't need someone to tell him what he saw below.

A massive fire was moving at a very fast pace over the wilderness terrain. At least one person had gone down in some sort of a crash, possibly injured or trapped by the flames or both.

As the pilot neared the coordinates where radar had picked up the parachute, he spotted something at his two-o'clock position. He turned the helicopter towards the object out in the distance.

As he looked closer, he now saw what he thought were multiple parachutes on the side of a small hill. It looked like there were three or four. He scanned the area for signs of life but didn't see any. The fire was rapidly approaching and the pilot estimated it would be to the parachutes in approximately fifteen to twenty minutes.

As he slowed, he counted four parachutes.

This is strange...

Whoever had used those parachutes was nowhere to be seen. The pilot looked forward and to the left and right. Then, approximately six hundred yards to the ten o'clock position, he thought he saw some wreckage.

Was that the aircraft?

The planes looked like small ultralights. The fire was burning out and around the wreckage. As the pilot flew almost directly over the craft, he realized that's exactly what they were. At least three ultralight craft crashed in the vicinity of each other.

"*There must be four*," he thought.

The pilot radioed back the information, and, as he was doing so, it started to dawn on him. There was no way that multiple aircraft would crash simultaneously and all of the pilots bail out in the same area. He turned and made another pass this time taking video and photographs with his cell phone.

"In addition to rescue, we need to notify the FBI and we need boots on the ground right now! I strongly suspect what I am seeing here is a coordinated attack. Whatever was carried on these ultralight craft must have started this fire. I repeat we need boots on the ground immediately, and they need to be prepared. This is a terror scene."

Three quarters of a mile away, the four Arabs huddled together in a hole under a big tree. All were nervous. The tree provided some cover but not a lot. Fires raged around them. They wondered when Agha would arrive.

One Arab was assigned to "glass" the area periodically to make sure they were not being pursued, and that the fire was not close. Moments before, he saw a helicopter flying over the area of the crash. Now the authorities would know they were here. It would be dangerous to move until the sun went down.

They had notified Agha of their success, and told him they would proceed to the rendezvous point, which was still another five miles up Trail Ridge Road in a remote clearing.

The Arabs realized that the winds were blowing away from their location. Agha had studied the terrain and wind conditions for the planned attack closely. So far, it appeared to be a perfect plan. The winds could change, but, for now, the fire was not a danger, at least not to them.

Agha let them know they would not stop until they reached them. Before they left the area, he had told them they had one more act to perform and only Agha knew what he intended.

Joe and Spencer were headed to Denver. Spencer was uncharacteristically quiet during the flight. He assumed it was nerves and her focus on the operation ahead.

Spencer was mulling all the events that had transpired recently. She had not slept well in months. The pace and strain of what they were doing had worn on her.

In truth, she hadn't and wouldn't tell Joe, the scene in the cave was still haunting her. She was not ready for the violence and aftermath.

In one instance, while taking a cat-nap, she was walking in the cave alone. Suddenly, the dead rose up from the cave, one by one, and lurched toward her. She tried to run, but it was like she was in molasses. Just before they would catch one would always yell out the same thing. *"Why did you let this happen?"*

She would awake in a cold sweat. This dream kept invading her mind a number of times, and she didn't know how to stop the hallucinations, but once this was over, she would talk to Joe about it.

Thunder Hawk called Joe.

"We are getting close to Estes Park. Get this, some of the hotshots died in the fire up there. One of them was a Dog Soldier. I remember him, but did not know him well.

Isha sounds like he is ready to repeat the cave scene again, up there!"

"Oh shit! Damn. What happened?"

"Winds just changed on them really fast. The fire caught them in a small canyon area. It was pretty bad. Joe, here is the other thing that's going on. We got information from a search and rescue operator. Some ultralight airplanes had crashed together in the wilderness. These guys set the fires, Joe and when I say these guys, you know who I'm talking about."

Joe paused and shook his head. "Yea, I do. Son of a bitch."

Joe put the phone on speaker so Spencer could listen in. "Are the bad guys still out there or did they go out with the planes?"

"No," said Thunder Hawk, "They're still out there. Search and Rescue saw the parachutes. They better pray that Isha doesn't find them before the feds."

Joe noticed something came across Spencer's face as she stared at the phone. He couldn't put his finger on it and would ask her about it later.

"Got it. We're enroute. Isha is going to need us to help track these guys down."

Already the FBI and other government officials were putting together a massive federal response, with agents set to comb the entire state of Colorado to find the persons responsible. SWAT and other units were on the ground searching, although the fire was limiting their range.

Spencer looked up from the computer research she was doing on her IPad as she called SAC Bowman:

"We are looking at conspiracy to commit acts of terrorism transcending national boundaries. Every one of the conspirators, aiders and abettors will be charged. That includes that son of a bitch, Bashir. Yes, that's right, this is death-eligible, and so everything must be done right. I need Title III roving authority also. We are going to find the Arabs, and we need to nail them all to the wall!"

SAC Bowman knew at this point that telling her to come back and not proceed would be like talking to a brick wall and, it may even be helpful to have her on scene to talk with law enforcement.

As he hung up, analysts were running into the situation room. Wiretap operators had intercepted a call. The terrorist Agha was enroute to Colorado. Bowman called her back and gave her the news.

"There is something else planned then, damn! We have to find them. Where are they?"

"We don't know yet, Maria. Any information that you obtain, let me know right away, out."

Spencer looked down at her IPad. In one of her old emails, there was a 2003 FBI 302, which contained a debriefing of a member of Al Qaeda. The man talked about plans to set massive wild-land fires throughout the southwestern United States. Someone had filed the report away and nothing was ever done with it.

Recently, major news outlets had reported on this incident, and there had been hints in the media over the years since, that terrorists were planning fire attacks.

The FBI had long listed arson as one of the top domestic threats. Over the decade period from 1999 to 2009, statistics on domestic arson were staggering, causing over three thousand five hundred deaths and over seven billion in property damage.

Al Qaeda had published an article in its English language on-line magazine, Inspire, calling for fires to be set across the western United States.

Spencer also had been briefed that in the treasure trove found by Navy Seals in Osama Bin Laden's compound, there were detailed plans for creating wild-land fires in the United States.

Yet, no one had ever put it all together.

Spencer was on a time crunch and needed critical details. She strongly suspected that there were political reasons why this terror link to fires had not been pursued more aggressively. Now, they had an actual crisis, and she was certain this fire and others would be linked to terrorism. This indictment may have to be broadened to include many others, she thought.

As she continued to read, Spencer found several articles on the Yarnelle Hill fire in Arizona, where nineteen hotshots had tragically died. The official information was that the fire was caused by a lightning strike. However, one terror group had taken credit for starting that fire and another in Nevada, as well as fires in Israel. The media sued to obtain investigative documents about what happened. Spencer believed that additional western United States fires were linked to terror, and she was rapidly assimilating information, which would bring these people to justice.

She sent emails to her contact at the Department of Homeland Security and requested any reports or studies of fire terror and names of any suspects or persons of interest who had information.

Spencer then sat back in her seat and thought about the course that this case and investigation had taken. It was astounding in some ways. Drug cartels have been smuggling terrorists across the international border for years. They have been hiding out in the interior of the country, including in the Navajo Nation, for who knows how long, just waiting for a signal to strike. This information that we had known about for a decade or more that terrorists intended to use fire as a weapon. Yet no one had put it all together. The big question of why started to percolate through her head.

While she had never been a "conspiracy nut" and was more practical and thought mainly in terms with prosecution, her legal mind and training could not help but point her in other directions. As always, she had to ask the question, who benefited from allowing these attacks to occur, with a "soft" link to terror that had never thoroughly been investigated or even taken seriously?

The insurance companies would pay out millions in claims, but rates would skyrocket any place where there was a remote chance of power station attacks or fires being set. In the end, the insurance companies would probably make money on the fires.

And the politicians? Why hadn't more been said or done about this? Of course, both political parties would now leap on this actual crisis and try and make whatever they could about it. Perhaps there would be a new "war" declared. Beginning with the "war" on drugs, these events tended to cause that type of reaction. While no one would say it, Spencer thought World War III was already under way and had been for some time.

"Terror" had just taken new forms over the years, and both sides believed they were right. Either way, a new clash was coming.

On a practical level, she knew that a lot of the backlash would be coming her way. The finger pointing would begin before the fires were extinguished.

Yes, she had been assigned to run this investigation, and yes, she had worked tirelessly on it, but no one would remember that in the end.

Bashir had completely misled her. He could have given the word, which might have prevented these fires and the deaths. It wouldn't have been the first time that a snitch was unreliable, and it certainly would not be the last, but this time it was just too costly. He would have to pay dearly for that.

The only thing that she could do now is to continue to work to bring all of the people responsible for the fire attacks to justice.

Spencer looked up in thought as the attendants indicated the flight was in its descent towards the Denver International Airport.

Joe leaned over. "Maria, you realize that you haven't said a word in the last hour? I didn't want to disturb you, but you look troubled. Seriously, are you ok?"

"I'm ok. I just want to get there and find these guys."

"Me too, me too."

Adorned in traditional battle paint, geared up with various long and short-range weapons, Isha and his men were drawing very close to the site where the fires had been started near Estes Park.

He would connect with Joe and the others and they would find the Arabs at last, including the one who had killed Asija.

CHAPTER 24

"While they are dealing with the fires, we will have our opportunity, Allah willing." Agha turned in the passenger seat and eyed the two West African jihadists in the back of the rental car.

Both nodded in agreement. Underneath their feet, the airtight containers containing the deadly Ebola-pox virus jostled slightly with the bumps in the road.

Begay glanced over at Agha and gripped the steering wheel tighter. They were in Denver and one mile from the Cherry Creek Shopping Center. Agha looked on with anticipation, as this was the site of the beginning of the final act.

Begay reflected to himself. He knew that what he was doing was very wrong. It was against the oath that he had sworn, to protect and defend.

They have never done right by Native Americans.

Begay's father was one of the men killed during the 1970's in acts of racism in Farmington, New Mexico.

This was the heyday of "Injun rollin'," where young white men would beat up Navajos as a rite of passage. In 1974, three white Farmington youths tortured, bludgeoned and killed three Navajo men and tossed their bodies into a canyon. Officer Begay's father had been one of the men who joined in peaceful protests following the killings. Clashes with police ensued and someone shot the elder Begay. No one was ever prosecuted for his murder.

He was only a toddler then and he never got to know his father. Ever since, he had harbored a great deal of anger.

He rationalized what he was doing was no different then what the white men had done to the Navajos during that time.

Begay slowed as they neared the mall.

The Cherry Creek Shopping Center is located in the heart of Denver. It is a premier, upscale shopping center that offers first-rate stores like Neiman Marcus, Nordstrom's, Macy's, and Tiffany & Co. It has an eight-screen movie theater and over one hundred fifty specialty stores.

Begay's contact, a rookie Cherry Creek security guard named John, waited for them in the parking lot.

John had recently joined the security team after graduating high school in Aurora and two years at a junior college studying criminal justice. He was green but very eager to get the job done.

Today, Cherry Creek bustled with activity. It was June and every major store had big summer sales.

Moms with teenage sons and daughters eagerly milled in and about the shops, snapping up deals. Lines to get into restaurants were overflowing. Kids were streaming into the movie theater in droves, ready to watch the newest summer blockbusters.

Begay pulled into the parking lot and stopped near the W1 entrance close to Nordstrom's. Approximately one hundred yards away, John saw them park.

He exited his car and walked towards Begay, Agha and his jihadists. Begay got out of the car and met the security guard halfway. He extended his hand.

"Thanks for meeting me." Begay said. "As I told you over the phone, we need access to the ventilation system to run a drill. For now, this needs to remain quiet. As we discussed, we need you to get us into the control room. We are testing the security procedures of the mall against possible terror attacks. This will take a twenty-four hour period. We appreciate your help."

"Thanks Officer. I can get you access to the control room. Then I will introduce you to the other security guards. If you need anything else during the drill let me know."

"We will call you. And again we appreciate your help. This is a dangerous time and we need to make sure that the security systems in major malls like this are adequate." Begay again extended his hand.

The security guard shook it. "Okay, follow me into the mall."

Begay turned and nodded to Agha and his men. He followed John to the entrance.

Agha and his men waited until Begay and the security guard were almost to the shopping center entrance.

Agha exited first, and then his jihadists followed. They grabbed the sealed containers with the viruses and placed them in Neiman Marcus shopping bags provided by the guard.

Agha took the lead and strode forward in the direction of Begay. The jihadists followed behind.

Begay and John walked through the entrance. Inside the mall, they walked side by side. They chatted about the large crowds and the sales and festivities.

Begay noticed that it was almost wall-to-wall people. *"It would not be too hard to pull this off,"* he thought.

Ahead of them, just past the restrooms, was the security control room.

Inside the control room, two security guards sat talking about the Colorado Rockies baseball team, their weekend and some girls that one of them had met at a downtown bar. Both munched on Subway sandwiches. They occasionally looked over at the computer screens, which showed various parts of the mall. People were packed in everywhere. This was a typical holiday shopping crowd.

A knock on the door caused the guards to look up from what they were doing.

They both glanced at each other to see who was going to get up first.

"Flip you for it."

"Nah, I got it."

One of the security guards rose from his chair. Just as he did, he heard a key turn inside the door and saw the doorknob rotate. The door opened inward.

"Hey guys, how's everything going?" John stepped inside the control room followed by Begay.

"Hey, John what's up? What, you missed us so much that you couldn't stay away. You aren't scheduled today are you?"

"No. That's funny. Yea, I knew it was pretty busy and wanted to stop by. Also, I was contacted by Homeland Security, this gentleman. They need to do a security check on the mall."

Begay flashed his badge quickly.

"Yes, that's right gentlemen, my name is Roland Begay. I am with Homeland Security due to FBI bulletins;

we are doing security checks across the country, starting with the busiest malls. I need access to this control room and to the ventilation system."

The security guard who had gotten up to open the door shifted nervously back and forth. "No one told us anything about a drill. No offense. We will need to clear this with our supervisor."

Begay nodded his head and looked at John. Then, without warning, he pulled his .40 caliber Glock from his holster and fired rounds into the chest of the first security guard and the head of the second. The gun popped multiple times. Both guards collapsed.

John stared in shock, first at the downed security guards, and then at Begay, who trained his handgun on John.

"Don't move. I won't hesitate to shoot you too. Sit down." Begay pointed his pistol towards the chairs where the other security guards had just been sitting.

John froze.

"I said move."

John slowly walked over and sat down. He mustered the courage to speak. "What, what are you doing? Holy shit man!" John looked down to the floor. "They are dying."

The security guards weren't moving.

"They are already dead. Call the other security guards into the control room, and if you signal them in any way, or your voice changes, I'll kill you."

"No man, come on. We don't need to do this. I don't know what this is about but ..." John wasn't able to finish his sentence.

The partially ajar door flew open into the control room. Agha and his two men stepped inside. Agha had his pistol drawn as well.

"Oh shit man. Oh shit." John now stared at the jihadists. He held his hands in the air. "I don't have any issue with you guys. Just let me walk and I won't interfere."

"Call the other guards." Begay's voice was icily cold.

John picked up the radio.

"Bruce, Gary, this is control. Do you copy?"

Thirty seconds went by without a response. Then the guards responded.

"Control, this is Bruce. We are here. Just standard crap. Walking around. Who is this?"

"This is John. I had to come in because of the amount of people in the mall."

"Oh ok, no one told us. Well that's great. We could use the help, John."

"Yea, Bruce I'm happy to hit the stores now. Do you guys want to take over control?"

"Sure, that would be a welcome break. Right now?"

"Yes." John swallowed hard.

"Roger that."

John put the radio down.

He stared at Agha and the Jihadists.

He turned to Begay and says, "Don't shoot those guys. They are good guys, with families."

"No, we just want to talk with them." Agha and the jihadists dragged the bodies of the two dead security guards to the back of the control room, out of sight of the door. They stood in the shadows. Begay stayed close to John, sitting on a nearby table, his gun by his side.

A short time later, Bruce and Gary opened the control room door and walked in.

"Hey John. What's going on ..."

Their eyes opened wide as they saw Begay and movement from the back. The guards tried to reach for their weapons but were too slow. Agha and one of the jihadists shot them, knocking them down instantly.

Begay picked up his firearm, pointed it at John and fired. John's face showed shock as the bullet entered his chest. He slumped in the chair and quit moving.

Agha and the jihadists looked at the computer screens. Thousands of people were walking around the mall.

Agha thought: *The virus will infect the vast majority and they will be sick before they know anything. When symptoms manifest, it will be way too late. Nearly all of these people will die. It will be a horrible death when their internal organs become liquid. People will bleed to death all over this city. They will have contact with many more thousands of people. Those people will also die. This will start a pandemic and will complete what I started. They will know how weak the United States is to respond. With the burning of the fires, and the spread of the disease, this plan will be complete.*

Agha looked around the room. Begay spotted a map of the mall. He grabbed the map and opened it. It displayed critical systems like the ventilation system and the door leading to the forced air units.

He found a set of several keys with labels on them in a closed drawer.

This is actually too easy.

Begay marked the location of the ventilation system door and pocketed the map. He and Agha and his men holstered their firearms.

Begay dragged the dead bodies to the back, and the men tried to hide them the best they could. He motioned, and they left and locked the control room. Begay and one of the men donned security uniforms from the security office. By the time the guards were found, it would be too late.

The group walked away from the control room carrying the Neiman Marcus bags with them. People streamed passed, oblivious to any danger. Young kids laughed and joked and sipped on their cokes. Several adults walked by looking harried and annoyed.

Approximately two minutes later, Agha and the group reached the ventilation system door.

Begay went through the keys, and found the one that was labeled ventilation. He inserted it into the lock, and the door-knob turned and he pushed the door open.

Begay and Agha and the others walked inside the room, closing the door behind them. They saw several forced air cooling/heating units connected to an extensive system of ducts. It was a closed air system, meaning that the air was re-circulated over and over throughout the mall. This was the perfect environment to release the virus. Being June, the air conditioning systems were in constant use.

Begay grabbed one of the Niemen Marcus bags containing the sealed container with the Ebola-pox and handed it to Agha.

He gave the other bag to the two African jihadists. They had taken off their masks and already knew what to do. Agha put his hand on both of their shoulders. He thanked them for completing the mission. Although Agha knew they were likely infectious, they embraced. He was a martyr already, along with his other brave men.

Agha and Begay turned and headed out of the room, back to the rental car and drove away from the shopping center.

The African jihadists waited thirty minutes in the control room as they had been instructed. They had barricaded the door with a chair. Their pistols were out and at the ready.

Very carefully, they removed the box container from the bag. One of the jihadists punched the key combination into the container lock. He carefully pried open the lid so as not to disturb the aerosol container inside. The container was intact and sealed with a protective cap.

The jihadist looked at his comrade and nodded. He slowly twisted the lid off the aerosol can. He breathed in and coughed uncontrollably for a bit, spewing fluid out of his mouth.

He turned to the first forced air unit. He lifted a lock/ latch and pried one of the sides of the duct off of the unit. He aimed the aerosol can and sprayed the contents into the duct. The powder became airborne inside.

The jihadist quickly sealed the duct, and the pump forced air through the duct, sending the Ebola-pox into the mall. As the unit pumped over and over, the deadly virus was sprayed further through the duct system to vents in the ceiling. Soon, viral particles would circulate throughout the shopping center.

They went to the next unit and repeated the procedure, continuing to spray the contents of the aerosol can into the ventilation ducts. When they neared the end, the jihadists sprayed the last bit of virus into the air in front of them.

They breathed in deep, taking the Ebola and Smallpox into their lungs. That would hasten their deaths.

They pulled their razor blades out of their wallets. They each cut their fingers and walked out of the control room, into the mall still teeming with hundreds of unsuspecting patrons. They separated, and as they walked, blood streamed to the floor around them. None of the shoppers seemed to notice. One jihadist headed to the bathroom first, as instructed. He continued to bleed as he approached the sink.

A man at the sink next to him noticed he was bleeding.

"Ah man, you ok? You need some help?"

The jihadist turned towards him and nodded. "Can you get me some paper towels?"

"Sure no problem."

The man turned around and pulled several paper towels from the dispenser. A few other men looked on.

When the man reached the jihadist to hand him the paper towels, the jihadist began a horrific coughing fit, coughing directly on the good Samaritan and turning to the other side and coughing on another man.

Then he moved quickly to the stall and vomited short of it, and then vomited inside the stall.

The bathroom quickly cleared out. The jihadist then went from stall to stall wiping blood on the commode stall locks. He coughed continuously as new people came in.

Then he slipped gloves on his hands and headed to a Mexican restaurant in the corner of the shopping center.

Meanwhile, the other jihadist had already been to an Italian grill in the shopping center. He coughed as he walked up and down the aisles of the restaurant. His condition seemed to be worse than his comrade. He too felt nauseous, and he felt fluid leak from his nose and eyes.

From the restaurant, he walked the halls of the shopping center, wiping his eyes and touching any surface that others would touch, including the rails of the escalators. He took his gloves off and bled, a small trickle, as he walked. Drops containing millions of Ebola virus particles hit the floor everywhere. Unbeknownst to any of the patrons, the Cherry Creek Shopping Center had just become the worst bio-terror site in the world and now teemed with Ebola and smallpox.

CHAPTER 25

Joe and Spencer deplaned and rented a vehicle. A couple of hours later, they arrived at Estes Park, near the scene where the ultralights crashed on the non-descript hillside. After several hours, the first responders had contained the fire. Now, Joe was on the ground searching for clues that would give him an idea of what had happened.

The wreckage was badly charred. However, there was some remaining evidence of the type of firebombs that were used to start the fires on the bottom of one of the ultralights. Spencer took several photographs.

Joe looked around the surrounding terrain, the charred wreckage, the still-burning fire in the distance, and the tiny details of the foliage that was still "alive." He began to think on what was happening. As he focused inward, he thought back to Afghanistan, to his training, to the medicine man, to his dream and the medicine man's warning.

This was it. Here he was in this moment, and it was the most important yet in his life. He searched inside himself to figure out what had happened, and what was going to happen. He summoned the medicine man who had started him on this journey and he asked a higher power to help him.

He could sense it. Something large and terrible and catastrophic was on the verge of happening. He had felt it before September 11.

The night before it happened, he had awakened in a cold sweat, to a horrible nightmare, in which thousands of unidentified faces were screaming out in unison. And then later, he watched the towers fall with everyone else who was watching television that terrible morning. Now, he felt that same sense of dread.

This is what he had seen earlier on Agent Spencer's face. He looked over at her. She seemed to know what he was thinking and nodded.

Joe and Spencer were on the move. They expanded outward from the crash scene in a standard grid search, and it did not take them long to pick up signs.

He noticed foot tracks and broken branches and disturbance of the ground one hundred yards distant from the crash scene. Although the fire had destroyed a great deal of the evidence, it had not destroyed it all. Joe used the sign to calculate the direction in which the group was headed.

They had assumed there were four of them from the number of ultralights, and they quickly confirmed this by the number of foot tracks.

As Joe and Spencer crouched down, reviewing the evidence, he pointed out the sign and told her his thoughts on the direction that the group of four walked.

The tracks and dirt displacement told him that each of the four was wearing boots and had a pack with considerable weight.

Spencer then switched on her IPad and did a quick search of any landmarks or places in the area where someone might hide.

The search yielded results. There were cabins near the area of the fires in Rams Horn Village Resort.

Spencer placed a call to the number on the website. She identified herself and indicated that she needed information on who had rented all of the cabins in the past month, and she needed that information right away.

The manager put her on hold and came back on a few moments later. He said it was going to take some time, and he needed to see her badge to make sure he could release the information. Rather than yelling into the phone, Agent Spencer calmed herself and said "we will be right there."

"Joe, I think this is it. They're there. We need to get there right now."

"Let's go. Also, we need to search around the cabins for any large areas of concentration of people," Joe said with his calm, confident tone that indicated he was feeling something.

Spencer typed in a few more searches, and an article popped up detailing Red Cross efforts in the aftermath of the Estes Park fire.

A Red Cross shelter had been set up for the survivors who had lost their homes and property, four miles away on the outskirts of Estes Park.

The main shelter was in an old, seldom used two story building, with a large basement area. Around the building, the Red Cross had also set up tents, with food and critical supplies. All persons who had been impacted by the fires were being encouraged to stay there.

"That's it!" Joe was emphatic. "They will hit the Red Cross building. That's where they're headed. They are staging at the cabin, but their destination will be the Red Cross Center!"

"Oh, my God, Joe." Her eyes betrayed desperation. She noticed that, on the road headed in the direction of the cabin, there were several cars and first responders and fire trucks. Time slowed, and she felt dizzy. "We have to go to the cabins first and confirm. Let's go."

Spencer snapped her iPad case shut and ran for her car, following Joe.

When they got in the car, she called Bowman to tell him the situation. She requested immediate UAV (unmanned aerial vehicle) and air support.

The Department of Justice had been using UAV's for years to secretly monitor suspects and operations. Within minutes, two UH-60 Blackhawk Helicopters and a UAV were launched from Fort Carson, Colorado.

Joe called Thunder Hawk. Seconds later, Isha and his men were headed for the Red Cross station.

Nearing the Red Cross shelter, ten men, including Agha and Begay, had abruptly left the cabin moments before and had worked their way down Trail Ridge Road.

Agha would release the next container into the Red Cross shelter ventilation system. It would quickly infect all the people in the building.

Victory is close now.

He thought back to his days of fighting in Afghanistan, repelling the Russians and the Americans, watching his comrades die. In the years since, he'd seen the struggles his people had endured, what he himself had lived through, the loss of many in his family, including his father to an American attack. Now, there would be revenge.

The penalty would be extracted from the Americans. It was destiny, and it was a message. The wars had not accomplished for the Americans what they set out to do. Instead of killing men like Agha, they had bred anger and hate, and it was implanted deep.

Agha gripped the sealed container tight. In a couple of weeks the news would cover the sickening outbreak. The suffering would be intense. Untold thousands of people in the mall, and in the Red Cross shelter, would be infected with the Ebola-pox. They in turn would infect untold thousands who would infect untold hundreds of thousands, and the world would know that Agha, and the others like him, could hit them any time and in the worst possible way.

Agha and his men stopped the car now and pulled off the road, not three hundred yards in the distance, there it was, the Red Cross shelter and tent city.

There were people everywhere. As Agha suspected, everyone was milling about, crying and shouting.

It was exactly the chaos that lent itself to what was about to happen.

Agha looked around the city and the surrounding terrain.

The tent city had been built up against a small ridge, likely for protection from the winds.

He looked off to the back of the ridge. It provided them cover and concealment for their approach. He signaled with his hands, and the group saw what he intended.

Crouching down, Agha and his followers begin moving parallel behind the ridge. As they got closer, they could hear the cacophony of voices of the faceless people.

These displaced persons weren't the enemy in a violent sense, but they were Agha's chosen vehicle to attack the enemy. As the group neared the top of the ridge, he ordered them to begin to crawl.

As they went to the ground and crawled forward to the top of the ridge, Agha now held the metal container tighter, turned over, and slid on his back, looking up at the sky, so as not to disturb the vials.

Over the vast Colorado sky, stars were coming out, as the sun dipped below the horizon. As far as the eye could see, there were beautiful, bright stars. A slight breeze was blowing. He thought it was an odd, peaceful backdrop for the scene that was about to unfold.

The jihadist immediately to his right put his hand on Agha's shoulder. They all stopped. He placed the metal container beside him and turned over onto his stomach. They were a couple yards away from the top of the ridge; they could look down the encampment. As they inched forward, Agha reached the top first. Leaning up, he peered over it.

Below he could see the Red Cross shelter building and several tents arranged in an orderly fashion, approximately thirty yards apart from each other.

FEMA and the Department of Homeland Security were managing the shelter. Each tent was large enough to house families. People were coming and going from the building and walking into the tents surrounding it. There were no guards, and it did not appear there was any security system. Agha smiled.

As he looked past the tent city in the dark, he could see the fire burning miles away. It would take them a long time to put out this fire. He spotted a woman with a young boy holding her hand. They walked to a tent and went inside. Agha suddenly panicked. He felt emotion at seeing the child.

Where did the boy go?

He was young, a small boy. Agha hadn't thought much about the virus killing small children, but it was an inevitable part of the mission.

Right? It would make an even greater impact when the news about the attack ran on all of the American's media outlets. But what is bothering me?

Agha shook it off. The mission was at hand.

After he'd had a good look at how the shelter was set up, he formulated his plan. Agha slipped back down from the top of the ridge and signaled for the men to gather close around him.

He told them that three man teams would form a perimeter around the tent city.

Agha and the three remaining jihadists would wait until the others were in position and then they would enter the Red Cross building, find the ventilation system, infect it, and then finish it all off.

Agha completed his instructions. They briefly embraced, knowing this was the final moment that they would see each other in this life, and then his men were off, slithering down the ridge, using the cover of the natural foliage, and working their way down and around the tents. In a few minutes they would be in place, and Agha would start his descent.

At the back of the city where the road ended, Joe and Spencer jumped out of their car.

With guns drawn, they jogged to the Red Cross shelter building.

Begay and the five jihadists took their positions around the city. There were so many people around they missed Joe and Spencer by seconds before they reached their intended posts on the perimeter of the tents.

Overhead, a drone scanned the ground. Two Black-hawk helicopters also circled the tents.

The jihadists crouched down low, while gripping their weapons tighter.

Agha and his primary guards pushed forward, down the ridge, straight for the shelter. Dressed in Western clothing, so as not to cause alarm, they breached the outskirts of the first several tents. No one paid them any attention.

Agha held the briefcase container as he walked by a family sitting at a picnic bench. He smiled, nodded, and they smiled back. A campfire burned nearby. Ahead of them, not one hundred yards away, was the Red Cross shelter building. Agha quickened his step, and his guards followed.

Then, right in front of him, was the boy again. He had stepped outside the tent. His mom was nowhere to be seen. Agha felt the same lump in his throat. He looked at his bodyguards and then to the boy. The boy was staring at him. He was small, no more than four feet high. His eyes displayed innocence.

The field. An explosion. His dad. Gone in an instant.
No!

Agha willed himself back to the mission at hand. He could not fail his dad. This boy would not suffer long.

What is it about this boy?

Agha changed course abruptly and walked to within a foot of the boy. One of the jihadists grabbed his arm and pulled but Agha shrugged it off. He reached out and put his hand on the boy's shoulder. Agha looked down into his eyes. The boy smiled up at him.

Agha felt a rush of emotion, something very intense in that moment. It stopped him.

The hand holding. His mom. A young boy. Wounded by a drone attack.

This boy wasn't much different from Agha.

"Would his life take the same path?"

Agha looked intently at the boy and his words came slowly. "Hi young man. Where's your mom?"

The boy hesitated. "She is inside. The fires are so big. Did you see them?"

Agha grimaced. "Yes, I saw them. Listen to me, I'm sorry, but you would do the same thing if you were in my place. You must understand that."

The child frowned and then looked down. Not knowing what to say, the child turned. He headed back towards the tent. Agha watched as the boy walked away. His bodyguard searched Agha for clues about what would happen next, and then violence erupted.

Agha's momentary pause from his mission cost him dearly. Isha spotted him with the young boy and began sprinting towards him. Thunder Hawk ran behind Isha.

Isha reached Agha the moment that the boy walked back inside the tent. He dove at Agha and slashed him deeply across his left arm. The knife dripped red with Agha's blood.

Agha jumped to the right and pulled his own knife out. One of the jihadists pulled a .32 pistol. As he tried to slash Isha's throat, he parried. Their knives locked. Agha slashed Isha's wrist.

He fell back a few feet and lunged at Agha, who dodged the attack. He lunged again and slashed Agha's left thigh. Blood oozed out of the wound.

Agha looked down and then redoubled his attack.

The bodies were moving too fast for the jihadist to get a shot.

Thunder Hawk watched in slow motion as he ran to help Isha. When he closed to within fifteen yards, he shot twice killing two jihadists. His gun jammed attempting to kill the last jihadist.

He threw it down, pulled out a knife, leaned forward and threw it at the last gun-wielding jihadist.

The knife buried itself deep in his neck. The jihadist dropped to the ground. Thunder Hawk focused his intention on Agha.

At the same moment, Isha lunged forward, and Agha grabbed Isha's right arm. Holding it in a tight grip, Agha slashed Isha's forearm, causing him to drop his knife. Then in one hideous second swipe, Agha swung upward and cut Isha's neck, slicing through the front of it. Blood gushed out of his neck in spurts. Isha instinctively grabbed his neck with both hands and fell to the ground.

Thunder Hawk, shocked to see Isha fall, paused and locked eyes with Agha. He raised another knife in a defensive posture. Agha stepped forward, his knife held high, and he bolted in the other direction, running back towards the forest area and into the still raging fire.

Thunder Hawk rushed over to Isha, who was holding his neck and the blood was seeping through his fingers. He ripped off his shirt, folded it in half and gave it to Isha to press against his neck. Isha grabbed it and held it tight.

People were crowding around. Thunder Hawk yelled for help. Isha was struggling to breathe. He leaned up and whispered to him, "You must go and get him. End this Daniel."

Thunder Hawk's eyes welled with tears.

Isha slowly reached behind his waist with one hand and mustered enough strength to grab a sash from inside his belt. He handed the sash and then his .45 Kimber to Thunder Hawk. The blood still oozed from his neck, but it was going slower now. "You are in charge now. Go and end this. You have learned what you needed to learn. You are on a better path, Daniel. Go and find him.

"For Asija, for your dad. For the Dog Soldiers."

Thunder Hawk stood and was off, running after Agha.

CHAPTER 26

Agha ran into a large meadow in the burning forest, off of Trail Ridge Road. Trees were burning everywhere in a wide circle. Noxious smoke billowed into the sky.

Through the smoke, he saw the top of a bluff. The bluff had a sheer cliff wall, which extended from a valley to a precipice on top. A stream ran through the valley below. The heat grew more intense. He continued to run hard. A tree cracked to his right, heaved its last, and then fell forward in a loud thud, fires still consuming it. Agha jumped and darted left around the fallen tree. He saw a path to a clearing towards the top of the bluff.

He pushed himself harder onto the path and raced towards the clearing. He held the briefcase in his left hand as he ran. In his right hand, he held a large curved-blade knife. He extended the blade high as he ran. Agha yelled out in exhilaration for the coming moment.

Behind him, Daniel Thunder Hawk's pace was measured. As he closed the distance, he held Isha's .45 pistol in his right hand. The sash of the Dog Soldiers flew in the air behind him.

A burning tree fell in the path in front of Agha. He stumbled and almost fell but caught himself with his sword arm and rose up almost immediately. Another tree fell in the same path to Agha's right. And then another. It seemed that this whole section of the forest was about to jump into a huge burning flame. The fires raged to the front, right and left sides of the path. Agha could not advance any farther. His only hope was to turn and double back and head around the inferno, and then run to the top of the bluff.

As he turned, Agha stopped abruptly in his tracks. There, twenty feet away, standing in front of him, like an apparition come to life, was one of the Indians. This was the same one Agha had encountered by the tents.

I should have killed him then.

Agha stared daggers at this young enemy. He was the final obstacle to the end of his plan.

Thunder Hawk held the .45 in his right hand and the sash in his left. Agha dropped the briefcase.

Agha roared at him, "It's over. You can no longer stop me, just as your leader could not. I will kill you just as I killed him and your other fighter. Save yourself. You can run, and I will let you go. This vial has the virus and its already broken now. It will kill you also."

Agha scowled as he took two steps forward.

Thunder Hawk had a range of emotions. Memories flooded his head. His dad, his rage, his fear, his mom and her kindness. He felt fear again. His training, the failed run, the stick fight, the sweat lodge. He then heard a voice in his head; it was his father's. Forgiveness. Strength.

You must not fail yourself.

Thunder Hawk scowled back. He stood tall before he rammed the knife into the soil directly below him. The earth accepted it almost as a gift. The sash of the Dog Soldiers blew backwards in the breeze.

"You will not pass." Thunder Hawk said as he held the .45 in his right hand.

Agha hesitated. He sensed the courage of this young warrior. "*No it was foolishness,*" he thought.

222

Agha reached for the Glock in his waistband, and let out a loud cry.

He darted forward and leaped in the air to gain speed. He pointed his gun at Thunder Hawk. He was too slow.

In an instant, Thunder Hawk stepped his left foot forward, aimed, and fired the Kimber .45, launching the round toward its target. It glided effortlessly through the air, and then sliced cleanly into Agha's forehead.

Agha fell to his knees six feet in front of Thunder Hawk, dropped the Glock and knife.

Agha's eyes went wide as he stared into the eyes of the Dog Soldier. The last man he would ever see on earth. His world went black as he leaned back and fell to the ground.

The sash fluttered ever higher into the sky.

CHAPTER 27

Before another shot could be fired back at the Red Cross building, two teams of Dog Soldiers swooped down from out of nowhere, behind the jihadists and Begay, and with guns drawn, ordered their surrender. Four of them, including Begay dropped their weapons, and the Dog Soldiers took them into custody. Four refused and the Dog Soldiers shot them dead.

Joe and Spencer moved through the crowd to help maintain order. Numerous jacket-clad federal agents arrived at the shelter moments before the shots went off.

Thunder Hawk emerged from the forest and walked towards the agents and the other Dog Soldiers. Federal agents with weapons drawn shouted and yelled. They ordered Thunder Hawk and the other Dog Soldiers to the ground.

The Dog Soldiers escorted the four Arabs to the center tent, weapons drawn. Spencer, at a full sprint, yelled for them to stop. She closed to within twenty yards of Thunder Hawk and stopped, putting her hand to her mouth.

He looked to his right and to his left and nodded to the Dog Soldiers. They each dropped their weapons. Thunder Hawk looked at the agents.

The agents pointed their guns at him and shouted "Get on the ground!"

He stared straight ahead at the agent closest to him and refused to break his gaze. The agent pointed his gun at Thunder Hawk's head. He did not flinch. Instead of dropping to the ground, he held the briefcase container in front of him. His gaze never left the agent's, then walked away from the agents and towards Spencer, his stride confident and composed.

As Thunder Hawk got closer and closer, no one fired. Something about his demeanor stopped them. She locked her eyes on Thunder Hawk's, and he did the same.

Within hand-shaking range, he stopped. Thunder Hawk reached out to Spencer, offering the container. She took it gingerly. He nodded with respect.

Thunder Hawk turned and signaled to his men, who were holding the jihadists and Begay. They pushed them in front of the agents.

When they reached Spencer, Thunder Hawk gestured and the Dog Soldiers backed away and ordered the Arabs to the ground. He turned custody of the terrorists over to Spencer.

Without another word, Thunder Hawk did an about face and walked away, oblivious to the stares and shock around him. The other Dog Soldiers followed. The agents who had their guns pointed moments earlier now lowered them to their sides.

They parted as Thunder Hawk walked through them. Joe Eagle stood a little taller from across the field and stood straight in awe and respect. Then he raised his fist in a moment of victory, and cried out. The Dog Soldiers quietly disappeared into the night.

Minutes later, Spencer handed the container to FBI Special Agents trained in bio-terror. They drove the container and its contents to Denver. Officials with the FBI and CDC then loaded them onto a highly secret military transport plane, on which they would be flown to the U.S.

Army Medical Research Institute of Infectious Diseases (USAMRIID), at Fort Dietrich, Maryland. There, scientists would study the contents of the aerosol container under the highest known biological security measures.

Spencer obtained critical information minutes after Thunder Hawk left. She called Thunder Hawk and asked him to meet her at the Red Cross building. There they interrogated Begay, who cracked.

He told Spencer about the events at the Cherry Creek Shopping Center, several hours before, and that they had released two jihadists and one of the briefcase containers with them.

"We went inside the control room and found the ventilation system. They emptied the containers containing Ebola, in some virus form. The jihadists were stricken with the Ebola virus already."

Spencer sprinted out of the building and called SAC Bowman. By the end of the short conversation, Bowman made emergency calls, which reached all the way to the presidential staff. The president ordered the Justice Department and the military to quarantine Cherry Creek Shopping Center, to lock it down and guard it. The President authorized the use of lethal force.

The military was also given authority to quarantine the entire city of Denver, if they believed it necessary. No one was to leave or enter the mall.

The Federal Emergency Management Agency (FEMA) and the CDC activated the National Incident Management System plan.

The plan for preventing a pandemic went into effect, federal officials made frantic calls back and forth between the various emergency management agencies, the military, Department of Justice and the Governor of Colorado. The Governor activated the National Guard and quick response forces at Fort Carson Army base.

Members of the guard, the local police, and scores of federal agents were ordered to the Cherry Creek mall. CDC officials boarded military transports and were in flight and headed to Denver. FEMA officials made calls to a pre-selected defense contractor, which suggested that McNichols Sports Arena would be a good place to serve as a temporary quarantine detention center.

Inside the Arena, the contractor would construct a series of air-tight, windowless buildings. Armed Marines would be stationed every five feet around the barbed wire fence.

Elevated guard stations, which would house a team of snipers, would be built at each corner around the fence. Each of the windowless buildings inside the fence would contain dozens of rooms inside, closed and hermetically sealed from each of the other rooms, using specialized glass and a series of doors.

These rooms would house the potentially exposed "patients" for the twenty-one day period in which the doctors would observe them to see if they had contracted the Ebola virus.

If at all possible, the doctors and CDC officials were to try to keep families together inside a single room.

CDC personnel, scientists and doctors would use a central room inside the building as a command center. It would contain a large computerized screen, with camera views of each of the sealed off rooms.

The plan was to quarantine everyone inside the Cherry Creek Shopping Center, until they could be transported, under heavy guard in large box containers, to the detention center.

Those who were hit by the virus would no doubt protest and be horrified, but it was a matter of national security and absolutely necessary to avoid a complete, worldwide pandemic. CDC officials at the detention center would vaccinate everyone potentially exposed to the virus, with a newly developed Ebola vaccine, and stores of smallpox vaccines, which the United States had stockpiled. The hope was that the vaccine would at least mitigate the damage that the viruses would cause.

Spencer was in her car and speeding to the Cherry Creek Shopping Center.

She had tears in her eyes, feeling that she had failed. Despite her best efforts, the worst thing imaginable had happened. Thousands would die horrible deaths. She heaved as she cried.

At the Red Cross shelter building, Begay pleaded with Thunder Hawk.

"I had to do it. You know how it is? The money, right Daniel? You were there. I had no choice. I gave you what you needed. Now you can let me go. I will say I took the gun away and escaped if they catch me."

Thunder hawk looked down and then up and shook his head. His eyes focused. He set his jaw, raised his .45 and put a bullet in Begay's head.

CHAPTER 28

A mother and her young son walked out of the front entrance doors of the Cherry Creek shopping center. The little boy was eating an ice cream cone. He smiled and looked up at his mom. A couple of teenage girls walked by them, headed into the mall, one texted frantically on her iPhone 6, barely watching where she was going.

As they opened the entrance doors, sirens began blaring loudly. The noise was growing. The mom looked towards the street, and grabbed her son's hand tightly. She leaned down and put her arms around her son and pulled him in close.

Dozens of police and military-type vehicles were descending upon the mall from every entrance. One police car screeched to a stop right in front of the mom. Two officers, guns drawn, jumped out. They wore masks.

"Freeze! Don't move! Stop right there!"

The mom was now kneeling on the walkway, too stunned to speak.

Why were they wearing masks?

"Ma'am, we have an incident. You are not in danger, but you are going to have to go back into the mall. Just get up and walk with your son back into the mall."

The mom was still too scared to speak. She noticed that the police officers were not moving closer to her. They still had their guns drawn. She slowly stood, holding her son's hand tighter. She looked at the officers and turned and began walking back to the mall entrance. She glanced back at the officers.

The mom and her son opened the entrance door and went back inside.

Similar scenes were playing out at all of the mall entrances. Police and National Guard members, wearing gas masks, now had the entire mall surrounded. Police cars were stopped, lights on, at every stop-light surrounding the mall and at every entrance and exit into parking lots surrounding the mall.

National Guard personnel, accompanied by police, were ordering anyone found in the parking lot or in their vehicles, back into the mall. The masks alarmed several people. One woman cried out asking for answers. The "party line" was the same. There were reports of a local gas leak, which could be dangerous, and the safest place for everyone right now was inside the mall. Some people protested, but remarkably, the officers were able to get everyone in the parking lot to go back into the mall, without use of violence.

Once the parking lot was cleared, the officers and National Guard personnel moved in towards the entrance doors around the mall.

Patrons were glued to the windows. They watched wide-eyed as officers, guns drawn closed in on the doors.

At one entrance, a college-aged man opened the entrance door and tried to ask the officers what was happening. The officers rammed the door with their shoulders, knocking the young man down inside the mall. The officers then wrapped a chain tightly around the double door handles and locked the chain tight. The officers slipped steel wedges underneath the doors, and at the top. This happened simultaneously at each of the entrances to the mall.

Inside the mall, fear and confusion were setting in. The young boy was crying in his mom's arms. Hundreds of patrons were making cell phone calls to relatives and friends, asking for help. Strangers were talking with each other, trying to get answers.

In one of the corridors, near Nordstrom's, a fight broke out. One of the jihadists touched a man's arm and coughed in his face. The other jihadist tried to do the same to his buddy. Both men were budding Mixed Martial Arts fighters, and both cursed at the jihadists. The jihadist threw a punch, which one of the men deflected. He tackled the jihadist and knocked him to the ground. Now he was pummeling him. His buddy laid out the second jihadist with one punch to his temple. Blood was spurting out of the downed jihadist's nose and he went limp as the man punched him two more times. The man got off the jihadist now, blood on his hands. He wiped his hands on his shirt. His buddy came over and grabbed his arm.

"You ok?"

"Yea fine. What the hell was that?"

"I don't know. Man, what a couple of idiots."

Onlookers did nothing. Security was nowhere to be seen. A couple of patrons shook their heads and told the men that "those guys" deserved it. The jihadists both remained unconscious, in the middle of the hall.

In other areas of the mall, people huddled together, talking, crying and searching for answers as to why they were locked inside the mall. Relatives and friends called. No one could figure out what was happening.

The media outlets were reporting on the quarantine. No one from any federal or state agency had any comment. The media was not allowed past the police line, which surrounded the entire mall. There was speculation as news helicopters captured government personnel in "bubble suits" walking in and around the mall grounds. One news station aired the possibility of a disease outbreak. Others quickly picked up on that idea and soon it was generally being discussed on every channel. National media correspondents descended on Denver.

The President announced through his staff that there would be an emergency press conference within the hour and that people should not need to speculate or panic. Within the presidential war room, the mood was very grim.

Some felt that an announcement of a serious disease threat and potential pandemic would cause rioting and widespread panic.

Others felt that the announcement had to be made quickly, and that it must include an order for all those who had been in the Cherry Creek Shopping Center that day, to confine themselves in their homes, where they could be assessed.

The CDC officials were running estimates as to the potential scope of the outbreak, but it was impossible to know until they had first found and contained all of the patrons who had been within the mall.

Several members of the presidential advisement team questioned whether an airborne Ebola virus was even possible or viable.

All felt that the quarantine had to be imposed, however, at least through twenty-one days, the incubation period for Ebola, to resolve any doubts one way or another.

The President and Department of Justice officials put law enforcement and military personnel on high alert in every major city across the country. Those emergency personnel who were not actively fighting the still-burning fires, were told to be ready to enact martial law and impose curfews, if necessary. The Department of Homeland Security implemented the National Terror Alert System and distributed information throughout the country that the current terror threat was imminent. The message was clear: terrorists were here and had struck again on United States soil.

Spencer stopped just outside the police line. Joe pulled up next to her. They proceeded quickly to the line and badged their way through.

Near the entrance to the mall, they located the commander of the overall operation, an FBI Special Agent from Washington, D.C., and a group of CDC officials.

Agent Spencer introduced herself and Joe Eagle. She began to brief them on all that had happened and what she had learned.

"The virus is a combination of Ebola and Smallpox apparently. It is a hybrid. The terrorists apparently figured out a way to make it airborne, or at least their scientists did."

The CDC Doctor shook his head. "Dear God, this means that ..."

"Right. Everyone in the mall has been exposed."

"Anyone who was inside and left the mall." The CDC official added.

The CDC official grabbed his phone and excused himself and called a confidential number that went directly to the Presidential war room. The threat was worse than they thought, and the President needed to know that before making his address.

Inside the mall, a family walked by the still downed jihadists. One was waking up. He coughed loudly and fluid spewed out of his mouth. He coughed again and again and his body shook violently.

The dad and mom of the family looked at each other and their two kids moved away. The jihadist groaned loudly and blood began leaking out of his ears and eyes.

"Oh my God, honey, he needs help." The wife put her hand to her mouth.

The dad approached the jihadist and leaned down to touch his arm. He reached for a pulse, and noticed that fluid was now leaking out of his nose. It was also bloody. The dad reached for his phone and called 911. The jihadist coughed and groaned again and rolled to his side and vomited.

The dad stepped back.

He leaned forward and put his hand to the jihadist's neck to find a pulse, if there was one.

What the dad did not know at that moment, however, was that the Ebola virus was dissolving the jihadist's liver and kidneys, and he was now leaking his organs out of his body. Minutes from death, his body was completely disease-infested and highly contagious. The other jihadist had already succumbed and he lay still in a pool of fluid. The dad breathed in and unknowingly took Ebola into his lungs.

The presidential announcement shocked the nation.

"You have heard by now in the media that a group of cowardly criminals have set a series of coordinated fires across the western United States. We have evidence to believe that the fires were a direct act of terror. We also now know and believe that these same terrorists or group of terrorists have launched a biological terror attack against a single target, the Cherry Creek Shopping Center. We do not have all the details of the attack at this time. I have directed all national resources to deal with this issue and I urge the public to maintain calm and to stay attuned to all developments. We are setting up a national hotline and call in center and we will have more information very soon ..."

With carefully crafted language, the President continued to try to mitigate the situation, telling the nation that they had the situation contained, and that it was limited to within the Cherry Creek buildings.

The president added that as a precaution, they were calling upon anyone who had been inside the mall that day to remain in their homes and to contact authorities for assessment and treatment.

The president assured the public that the terror threat appeared to be eliminated, through the coordinated work of the FBI, Homeland Security and the military.

The President ended with a call to the citizenry to remain calm but vigilant, and to not attempt to obstruct the emergency personnel who were still working to extinguish the fires and to contain the damage.

The announcement flew through the mall, from one patron to the next. Fear swept through them like a tsunami.

Patrons banged on the mall exit doors and screamed and yelled. One man grabbed a speaker from the Apple store and ran at one of the exit doors and threw it hard at the window. The window cracked. An officer shot through the glass, killing him. People screamed and backed away from the exit. The officer, as instructed, quickly patched the hole with layers of plastic and tape.

Officers on loud speakers shouted messages into the mall at each exit door warning persons who might attempt to break through, that they would be shot if they did so. The officers told them to wait and that they would leave soon.

Inside, people lay down, exhausted and scared, in stores and in the hallways. They raided the restaurants inside the mall for food. Families and friends huddled together, but otherwise people mainly kept their distance from one another.

Nightfall came, and some slept. The majority, though, lay awake all night, shaking and crying with fear, anger and depression.

Spencer and Joe continued to talk to whoever would listen to try and help with logistics, background information and whatever else they could do. Spencer fought back feelings of helplessness.

She went from CDC "big wig," to police commander, to FBI Special Agent, pleading to be brought into the loop on the planning of the operation, to try and save the people in the mall. Spencer had an idea that the quicker the authorities could introduce sunlight into the mall, and fresh air, through whatever method, including knocking holes in the roof, the better chance of killing the airborne virus and saving the people.

The mall patrons were being exposed to the airborne particles, and no doubt in the end, they would all likely contract the deadly disease, without some plan. Again and again, she was rebuffed.

236

Another day passed with no incidents inside or outside the mall. Then, on the day following, the contractor sent word that the first of the buildings inside the quarantine center was constructed and ready to be occupied.

Officers around the mall announced that they would start moving people out of the mall, to a temporary structure, where they would be evaluated.

The first group to be moved would be families with children under ten years old. The officers announced that they would move people in groups of ten to fifteen people, from each exit, and that they would be given "bubble suits" to wear.

They asked the people inside the mall to maintain order and to allow the families with young children to form a line near the various exits.

Within the hour, CDC authorities, accompanied by armed officers, transported the first eight groups of people, for a total of ninety-four people.

Approximately thirty miles away, at a secret location, CDC and medical personnel waited for the detainee's arrival.

When the first groups got there, detention center employees wearing protective bubble suits escorted them off the trucks and into the compound and building.

Soldiers, also wearing protective masks, stood guarding the entrance and exit points.

The employees took the families with children into their assigned rooms within the building. Once inside the sealed rooms, the "patients" were allowed to remove their suits, with the assistance of CDC personnel.

Every four to five hours, medical personnel brought them food. There were large containers of water set up in the corner of the rooms. Otherwise, the rooms resembled normal hospital rooms, with beds, a small bathroom, a sink, and a satellite radio. CDC officials began administering the vaccines as patients arrived.

Over the next week and a half, as additional buildings were constructed, the CDC continued to move people from the mall to the CDC camp. Through the tenth day, no one had yet shown signs of contracting the virus, and everyone had their fingers crossed that the idea of an airborne Ebola virus or combination Ebola virus, was impossible, and that, if it was possible, that the vaccines would work.

Then the eleventh day came. The younger boy, of one of the original families to be transported, started coughing. Slowly at first, he coughed, and then the coughing got more intense and rougher, harsher, and more painful for him. He cried intermittently and gasped.

He tried to smile but he was rapidly developing signs of a serious disease. His skin darkened, and looked to his parents to be charred or black in color.

Blood vessels hemorrhaged inside him everywhere, and he bled, profusely. Black, unclotted blood seeped from his nose, ears and eyes.

His parents and older brother cried and held him while the boy slipped away. The virus' ruthlessly destroyed the lining of his throat, stomach, intestines, and organs. Then he died. And his brother and parents followed soon thereafter, in excruciating pain, emotionally and physically, as they watched and endured each other's death.

They were the first, but they would not be the last. Over the next two weeks, as a horrified nation waited for news, more would die. CDC could not transport the afflicted quickly enough. Many died in the CDC camp.

Others died in the Cherry Creek mall, waiting to be transported.

The virus killed forty-five percent of the people who were in the Cherry Creek Shopping Center that day, for a total of one thousand seven hundred ninety four people. Yet, it could have been worse.

A very lucky fifty-five percent survived, which CDC credited to the vaccines and the grace of God and because of the information acquired by Spencer and Thunder Hawk from Begay, the quick response and lock down of Cherry Creek, along with the use of the vaccines, the death toll and pandemic were contained.

Only a handful of other people who had been in the mall that day, and who had left before the mall was locked down, contracted the virus and died.

The authorities were still searching for one family, who apparently had been in the mall briefly, and had boarded a plane for Costa Rica that afternoon.

CDC number crunchers estimated that the pandemic could have easily gone national, and even international, with a death toll in the hundreds of thousands if not millions, before the spread could be stopped.

Aside from the one stray family, however, the Ebola outbreak appeared to be totally contained.

Yet, the terrorists had claimed lives, and to some extent had won, and that was what was haunting Spencer in the aftermath.

CHAPTER 29

EPILOGUE

Six months later, authorities had completely contained the fires.

Remarkably, none of the members of the family that flew to Costa Rica had contracted the virus.

The Ebola threat had ended.

Yet, the attack by the terrorists in Colorado resulted in the horrific deaths of almost four thousand citizens.

In the aftermath, Spencer's life was tumultuous and uncertain. She was constantly on the move, with debriefings from this agency and that agency, the FBI Director, and members of Congress.

The president summoned her and Joe to the White House. In a secret ceremony, the president gave each a presidential medal for civilian valor and a check for one million dollars.

The checks were cut from a presidential discretionary fund, through an anonymous bank, from a "black" account. The public would never know about their contributions, or those of the Dog Soldiers.

Joe Eagle took some time off to fish in Montana. He meditated as he sat by the river. He threw his fly line in and watched it float across the calming waters. It felt good when the line tensed and he hooked a fish. He wasn't drinking as much these days.

He pondered leaving the criminal investigations job and opening up his own private investigation agency. The Department of Homeland Security and the Drug Enforcement Administration had reached out to Joe, saying they had heard from FBI Agent Spencer.

They told them that there might be some contract work in Central and South America.

Spencer called Joe out of the blue. He was surprised, but happy. She wanted to see Joe. She had just run the Los Angeles marathon, posting her personal best time. Work had been busier than ever, but rewarding. Joe congratulated her and talked of his plans. They agreed to meet in Albuquerque for dinner in a week.

"I wanted to tell you that I am going to be gone for a while. Down south. Some things with DEA and Homeland Security we're going to be working on. I may give you a call, Joe. You never know."

"That sounds really interesting. What are you going to be doing?" Joe was cautiously intrigued. This last adventure had been a little much.

Well, I could tell you, but then we would have to kill you," Spencer deadpanned.

"Oh, I get it, I'm no longer in the *club*!" Joe teased her back.

"Never know, Joe, we may need to call you for help! Like rescuing us down there!"

Joe had to smile at that.

"Oh, no, my days of chasing terrorists and running through canyons are over. It was fun while it lasted, but anything you guys need, you know you can always call me."

"Yes I know. It's good to talk with you again, Joe. Take care."

"You too, Maria. Keep your head down, and thanks."

"Thanks for what?" Maria asked.

"We both got each other through the cave and everything else. You showed courage and it made me deal with some of my nonsense. We made it through the end, you know, how bad that it was."

Maria paused to let that thought sink in. "Anytime you want to talk Joe, just let me know."

In southeastern Montana, in the Northern Cheyenne Indian Reservation, Isha, Daniel Thunder Hawk, and a number of other Dog Soldiers participated in a traditional ceremony.

After months of medical care and rehabilitation, Isha had completely recovered. Rumors in Indian country were that he had come back from the dead. Whatever had happened, he was back, alive and well, and in charge of the warriors.

They fasted for several days and visited with a medicine man who performed a traditional cleansing ceremony. Isha told Thunder Hawk that this was an unusual moment in his life. He would today join an ancient and unknown sect of the Dog Soldier society, which had one mission: to protect their people.

Family members and friends came out to pray and support them. Wood and medicines were gathered in the traditional manner. Dog Soldiers set the site up, made offerings, and a feast was prepared. This was an important Sundance Ceremony.

The community knew about the events involving the terrorists and the heroic deeds of Isha and the Dog Soldiers.

The Cheyenne were proud. Thunder Hawk was about to be formally added to the Dog Soldier society. In so doing, he would offer his personal journey as a prayer, atonement for himself, his family, his Dog Soldier brethren, and community.

After the ceremony, Isha planned to rejoin his Dog Soldiers, and avoid further involvement in the affairs of the federal law enforcement agencies, to the extent that he possibly could. The next phase of his life, at least for a while, would be quieter, and he would teach some of the younger Dog Soldiers. He had earned the right to some peace.

Unfortunately, peace would be elusive. Winds of change were blowing in Washington, D.C. In the aftermath of the terrorist attacks, the FBI, Department of Justice, and presidential staff convened several "high level" meetings to attempt to understand the failures and weaknesses that led to the attacks and the agencies' failure to stop them.

Of course, the usual post-catastrophe actions had already been taken: the FBI "retired" SAC Bowman, and told Agent Spencer that she would head to Central America and Africa to take up another investigation.

Before she left, she was ordered to attend, what would prove to be a particularly painful meeting with Department of Justice and presidential staff.

The meeting began in a relatively normal after-action format, with the various 'big wigs' trying to figure out what went wrong and who to blame.

She calmly walked them through the events from start to finish, answering questions along the way.

The meeting turned, however, at one point, when one of the members questioned her about the terrorists' ability to hide in the Navajo Nation for years without detection.

She protested that they had also discovered terror sleeper cells in Colorado during the course of the investigation, but the committee wasn't hearing it. Soon, the debate was lively and blame was focused on the Native Americans.

"Isn't it also true Agent Spencer that the FBI was obstructed during its investigation by the Native Americans who interjected themselves in the search?" The committee member glared down at her.

"No, that isn't true at all. In fact, they were instrumental in apprehending ..."

"Agent, they obstructed the investigation, and you were the one who pointed this out. We have SAC Bowman's notes. Do I need to remind you of what you said?"

Spencer silently seethed and knew where this was going. She was being used. This wasn't about a fair and full airing of the facts to figure out what could be done to change for the better. No, this was a witch-hunt. This was about blaming Native Americas for the FBI's failures.

"Agent, would you agree that it was much easier for the terrorists to hide in the reservations because of the lax law enforcement presence there?"

"No, I wouldn't agree with that at all. I would say that..."

No one bothered to hear her explanation. Instead, the committee members shuffled some paper and put their pens down.

"Agent, we appreciate your time. You are excused."

The committee sat in stony silence, all eyes on her, waiting on her reaction.

She didn't give them the satisfaction of looking stunned or hurt. Instead, she smiled, grabbed her files, raised her head, and with confidence, walked out of the room.

ABOUT THE AUTHORS

Jason Bowles is an attorney in private practice and has been trying criminal cases for over twenty-years. In 2013, he started his own practice, The Bowles Law Firm. He is a former federal prosecutor, and now a defense attorney. He has handled cases involving narcotics, immigration, and national security on the United States-Mexico border. Some of his most interesting cases have involved Native Americans from the Navajo Nation and throughout New Mexico's pueblos.

Lawrence Trujillo served as a United States Marine in Vietnam. His career extended thirty-five years in law enforcement and as a private investigator and security specialist with two national laboratories as a contractor with the United States Department of Energy. He investigated capital case violent crimes, many related to drug trafficking and homicide throughout the Southwest, to include numerous cases on Indian lands in New Mexico, Arizona, and Utah. As a member of defense teams he investigated cases involving "national security."

Both call New Mexico home.

www.ingramcontent.com/pod-product-compliance
Lightning Source LLC
Chambersburg PA
CBHW050415260626
47156CB00003B/1018